My Brother's Keeper

My Brother's Keeper

Matthew Edwards

Writer's Showcase
presented by *Writer's Digest*
San Jose New York Lincoln Shanghai

My Brother's Keeper

Writer's Showcase
presented by *Writer's Digest*
an imprint of iUniverse.com, Inc.

For information address:
iUniverse.com, Inc.
5220 S 16th, Ste. 200
Lincoln, NE 68512
www.iuniverse.com

ISBN: 0-595-15213-9

Printed in the United States of America

Dedicated to my wife whose love and commitment is responsible not only for the completion of this book, but for the completion of my life. I love you Goose.

Prolougue

The snow continued to flutter effortlessly throughout the evening. With the first light of dawn filtering through the partially drawn blinds in Adam's bedroom, he stared out the window with barely suppressed excitement. Not only was it the first snowfall of the season, it was occurring on Christmas morning.

With great anticipation he squinted his eyes with fierce determination and studied the ground for the slightest indication of hoof prints or sleigh marks. His failure to detect any physical proof of Santa's arrival did little however to dampen his spirits. After all, everyone knew Santa's reindeer landed on the roof.

It was only five-thirty in the morning and he still had another thirty minutes before his grandmother would arrive to unlock his bedroom door and perform her morning ritual. Still thirty minutes before he could set his eyes upon the most magnificent sight ever witnessed. Thirty infinitely, long minutes before he could see the gifts Santa left him by the fireplace.

Though he knew the outcome, he couldn't resist the urge to quietly check the locked doorknob of his bedroom door. From countless previous attempts he knew the deadbolt on the other side would be engaged, but still he had to try. The solid oak door resisted his attempt at manipulation and Adam simply accepted the fact he was going to have to be patient. It didn't matter though. He'd waited this long for a visit from Santa; he could wait a little longer.

In the four years he had lived with his grandmother, their farmhouse, for whatever reason, had not been on Santa's chosen route. But Adam knew this year would be different. It *had* to be different. Though he was not allowed to visit Santa last month at the mall, he had been able to sneak eight letters into the mailbox down the street from his bus stop. Each letter, addressed to Mr. Santa Claus, 1225 Christmas Tree Lane, The North Pole, had contained a simple list of presents and directions to his house from the North Pole. His list contained only three items, a red sled like his friend Jimmy's, a pair of warm mittens, and a backpack to carry some of his books to and from the school bus.

Adam looked again at the small alarm clock on the desk next to his bed. Still twenty minutes to go, he thought. Maybe being Christmas morning, she'll surprise me with an early visit, he thought optimistically. Maybe I'll be allowed to open my presents before the chores.

My presents, he thought wistfully.

Adam removed his tattered green pajamas from his thin, frail body and placed them neatly into the hamper beside the locked door. He pulled on his heavy wool underwear, a pair of faded jeans, and a pullover sweat shirt, before giving his hair a final sweep of the brush, eventually getting it settled into place. He was determined to please his grandmother this morning of all mornings. Rinsing his toothbrush in the nearly frozen basin beside his nightstand, he scrubbed each tooth as if one might produce the genie from Aladdin's lamp. Finally, he pulled on his socks and tied his boots before tucking his sweatshirt into the jeans. Studying the result in the cracked mirror hanging on the wall, his pale blues danced with a mixture of pride and relief. Even the dark black and blue his grandmother had inflicted under his left cheek was barely noticeable. Today was going to be a great day, he thought to himself.

While he made his bed, being sure to pull the corners as tightly as possible, he began to hum his favorite Christmas carol. Not loudly though, since singing was not permitted in the house. Other than reciting biblical passages and performing countless chores, there weren't *many* things that were allowed in his grandmother's house, he realized.

With his bed as tight as any marines, he knelt down beside it, folded his hands, and bowed his head.

"Dear Father in Heaven," he began, "please forgive the awful sin that I have committed. Though I am not worthy of your love, I pray one day for your acceptance. I humbly ask that you bless my grandmother, who is both loving and kind."

Though he doesn't fully understand the concept of sin, his grandmother forced him to relegate the prayer to memory years ago. Not a day passed without him being reminded someone named Satan had already claimed his soul.

Before he stood, he paused to add a prayer of his own. "And God, please, please, please let Santa understand the directions I gave him. Amen."

Finally, at five fifty-nine, he heard his grandmother's heavy footsteps ascend the stairs to his bedroom. The excitement, which overwhelmed him earlier, increased tenfold with each echo of her step.

Wait till Jimmy sees my new sled, he thought.

As the keys jingled outside the door, Adam assumed his position to the left of the bed and stood as erect as his back would allow. Nothing could ruin the happiness and joy he felt this morning. His room was spotless, his clothes neatly placed in the hamper, his bed made, and his appearance groomed.

My first real Christmas, he thought.

My first real presents from Santa.

As the rusted hinges of the door squeaked inward and his grandmother stepped inside, Adam smiled broadly and gushed, "Merry Christmas, Grandmama!"

The old woman flashed him a cold stare and the permanent scowl of her face deepened.

"I've told you before there is no such thing as Santa Claus and certainly no such thing as Christmas for children as wicked as you. Now get outside and feed those damn animals while I inspect this pigs sty you call a room. And make sure that barn door gets closed this time," she slurred angrily, the stench of last nights liquor still permeating her breathe.

Adam stood frozen in fear and disbelief. How could this be true? How could this be happening? Everyone he knew got a visit from Santa Claus. Every year they showed off the toys and gifts they received for their year of good behavior. What had he done that had been so bad as to banish him from Santa's list forever? His eyes began to fill with tears and he bit his lower lip to keep it from trembling, but his grandmother had seen it all before.

"Why you ungrateful bastard," she hollered, taking a step toward him. "If it wasn't for my kindness in letting you stay here, they would have kept you locked up too."

She reached him just as she finished the sentence, and with speed and force uncharacteristic of a woman her age, slapped him across the face. "Now get outside and start those damn chores!"

His face burned, as if touched by a match, but Adam knew better than to stand there and cry. He ran past his grandmother, down the stairs, and out the front door, all the time wishing she were dead.

Once outside, the cold air quickly numbed the pain in his cheek. He walked slowly toward the barn, taunted by the crisp crunch of snow beneath his boots. Snow that, without a new sled or a warm pair of mittens, served only as a cruel reminder of his disappointment. At that moment, he hated the snow.

He hated his grandmother.

He hated Jimmy for having a sled like the one he wanted.

But most of all, he hated his parents for dying.

Forty minutes later he finished sweeping the stalls, raking the muck, and feeding the animals. Dreading the sight of snow, but not wanting to be late for breakfast, Adam headed back outside. He knew his grandmother would find at least a dozen things wrong with his chores, but this morning he just didn't care. All the spankings, all the verbal abuse, even all the time he'd have to spend in the dark, cold basement, couldn't compare to the misery he was feeling at that moment.

Suddenly a strange noise, like somebody crinkling aluminum foil, only louder, brought him out of his zombie-like trance, and he glanced in the direction of the sound.

At first, the sight was so bizarre he was sure the snow's reflection or the glare of the sun was playing tricks with his eyesight. But a moment later, the image was clear and there was no mistaken what he saw.

The farmhouse was engulfed in flames.

He ran to the front yard, but was unable to get any closer than the brick walkway. Even from that distance, the searing heat of the fire made it difficult to breathe. Terrified at the sight of the blaze, Adam looked about, first for help, then for his grandmother.

Her faint screams were barely audible above the crepitating roar of the flames. Trying to focus on the sound of her voice, Adam glanced toward the attic, simultaneously shielding his eyes from the thick smoke and the glare of the sun.

He saw his grandmother frantically banging on his bedroom window, trying desperately to get it open. As he watched, paralyzed by panic and indecision, he saw her pulled from view and another figure appeared in her place.

A very familiar figure.

Smiling down at him from the flame engulfed room, Adam saw himself.

CHAPTER *One*

The ultra-violet rays of sunlight had somehow found their way through the tightly drawn shades in Adam's bedroom. Though his eyes were closed and he remained somewhere between much needed sleep and a harsher reality, Adam knew before the alarm clock sounded that another workweek was about to begin. Unable to ignore the intrusion of daylight any longer, he gave into the dawn's early morning light, blinking and squinting until his eyes could handle the sun's assault.

Sitting up slowly he reached for the matches on his nightstand, lit a cigarette, and took a deep, satisfying drag. Holding it in his lungs much longer than necessary, he exhaled a massless cloud of smoke toward the vaulted ceiling of his bedroom. He knew it was a disgusting habit, but also one he wasn't quite ready to quit. It had become a crutch during his final and most difficult year of law school. He almost felt he owed a debt to the Marlboro Man, which could only be repaid through the contamination of his lungs.

Taking another drag, he swung his legs over the bed and noted rather begrudgingly the luminous green lights of his alarm clock flashing 5:45 AM. In fifteen minutes the Mr. Coffee Maker would automatically begin perking three very strong cups of coffee, two of which he would drink before leaving the house, and the third sipped during his commute downtown.

Mr. Coffee Maker and Mr. Marlboro Man, where would I be without you guys, he thought.

He let out an involuntary groan as he stood and stretched his lean frame from side to side. His entire body felt as though it had been on the losing end of a steel cage-wrestling match. His back was stiff, his head throbbed, and his eyes were bloodshot. It had been another restless night spent in the bizarre realm of his subconscious. Another night of waking to a backdrop of sheer blackness terrified beyond belief. In his mind he was screaming, but somewhere along the way fear had cut the message to his vocal cords. He awoke to the taste of perspiration on his upper lip and the night air chilled his clammy skin. He spent several frightened minutes listening to his rapidly pounding heart; sure the organ would burst through his rib cage at any moment.

The next few hours he desperately tried remembering some aspect of the nightmare which had once again robbed him of a good night's sleep.

A blood sucking vampire, a two-headed monster, drowning in a lake or falling from a cliff. Any memory lending credence to the fear and horror that burrowed its way deep into his subconscious mind upon waking would satisfy his need. But whatever demons lurked in the dark corners of his mind managed to find their way back into oblivion, leaving him as frustrated as he was frightened.

The nightmares had been dormant for so many years Adam couldn't help wondering what caused them to re-surface now. As a child, he suffered horribly at night from the visions played out in his dreams. Unlike other children, his boogey-man wasn't hiding under the bed or neatly tucked away in a closet. Rather the source of his fear laid somewhere deep in his sleep. He remembered the dread that befell him as evening approached. The heavy weight of anxiety that cloaked him like a wet blanket as the time for bed neared. Regardless of the effort he put into *not* sleeping, it always found him, and sooner or later so did the nightmares.

In the beginning, he had been examined by several child psychologists but to no avail. Not only was he unable to remember the nightmares, but to complicate things further, he had no memory of his life before the age of eight. He knew his real parents had been killed in a car accident and he knew he had been in a coma for six months as a result of that accident. But his awareness of these facts came from outside sources rather than from actual memories.

At the age of eight, his first real memory was that of waking in a hospital room surrounded by strangers and unable to recall his own name. His entire existence prior to the accident was an unknown quantity and remained such twenty years later.

After three months of testing, prodding, poking and analyzing, the psychologists at the hospital declared he was a true amnesiac with no known relatives or friends of the family. If it hadn't been for his subsequent adoption several months later by Neil MacGregor, Adam wasn't sure how his life would have turned out.

About a year after the adoption, his nightmares suddenly stopped. On rare occasions he would suffer a nightmare or two, but they were few and far between and he could deal with their infrequency. Now, the nightmares were averaging about four a week.

Trying to refocus his thoughts from the nightmare, Adam let his mind drift to the events surrounding the past weekend instead. At a party Saturday night in honor of his passing the bar exam, he had somehow gotten himself engaged to his longtime girlfriend Allison Allsworth. The momentous announcement, made by his future father-in-law, Senator Robert Allsworth, had caught Adam completely off-guard. Before he could register a reply, the announcement had taken on a life of it's own with friends and family congratulating him and telling him how lucky he was. Sure he and Allison had discussed marriage in the past, but Adam thought it was in the same way Bostonians discussed making it to the World Series. They were sure it would happen someday, they just didn't know when. Soon Allison was telling the guests *they* had already selected her ring and had had it sized at the Jeweler's Building in downtown Boston. She then proceeded to tell him not only where the building was and whom he was to see, but had also taken great pride in telling everyone how much the four-karat diamond was going to cost. Adam wasn't sure what frightened him more, the nightmare or the engagement.

He stretched again, rotating his head clockwise on his shoulders. "Stress," he said. "It's just stress," he added for reassurance, as he headed for the bathroom. He hoped a hot shower would steam away some of his weariness and his friend Mr. Coffee Maker could take care of the rest.

At 6:15, his hair still damp and his bones still weary, he stood in front of his mirror comparing his favorite blue pinstripe suit to a dark chocolate Brooks Brothers suit Allison had insisted he purchase. With little thought, he selected the pinstripes and also an appropriate tie to match.

At 6:43, his hair dried but uncombed, he stood in front of the same mirror wearing khaki beach shorts, a loud Hawaiian shirt, and a pair of open toe sandals. His appearance would have been comical if it weren't for the fact he had no memory of the past twenty-eight minutes. Just as upsetting as his current attire was the ten-inch butcher knife he clutched tightly in his right hand.

Dropping the knife, he staggered back from the mirror and sat clumsily on the bed. Staring in disbelief at his hands, he noticed for the first time he was bleeding. Whether from shock or fear or perhaps both, he also noticed for the first time the two words scrawled repeatedly in blood across his mirror:

HE'S COMING!
HE'S COMING!
HE'S COMING!

CHAPTER *Two*

"I told you I no longer want any part in the project. I want out!" Senator Allsworth whispered firmly into the receiver. "I'm not going to tell anybody about anything. For God's sakes, I have just as much to lose as you or anyone else connected to the Organization."

"Senator, I'm afraid your resignation is no longer an option," the man on the other end replied calmly. "Too many people with a great deal more influence than you'll ever have as a senator simply will not allow it. For more than twenty years now the Organization has single-handedly guaranteed your seat in the Senate. Our investment of time, money, and resources is too great to simply allow the relationship to end."

"Jesus, Mary and Joseph, hasn't the Organization seen the latest polls. Congressman Oliver has a four-point lead with only two months until the election. If the press finds out about my association with you, re-election will be the least of my problems."

An eternity seemed to pass before the other man finally spoke again.

"Senator, my associates and I are well aware of the polls and of our personal interest in your being re-elected. Trust me Senator, the Congressman's bid for your seat is about to take a very nasty turn. And as far as you're concerned, unless your loyalty and silence to our Organization remains status quo, you're right about the election being the least of your worries. Have a nice day Senator."

The man hung up abruptly and Robert Allsworth remained seated with his eyes closed for several minutes before finally doing the same.

For more than three decades he had enjoyed a successful and rather profitable tenure as Massachusetts senior Senator. Since 1960, he had been virtually untouchable in the political arena. His opponents were usually weak and obligatory, assuming the Republicans even brought an opponent forward. On the rare occasion when a viable opponent did appear, the Organization arranged for some statewide scandal to surface which caused the campaign to dissolve almost overnight. The Senator had no doubt one such scandal was in the making for Congressman Oliver.

He rose slowly from behind his desk and walked toward the wet bar like a man carrying a great weight on his back. He removed a glass and filled it with two ice cubes and a stiff shot of scotch. His first drink was arriving earlier each day. Bringing the glass to his lips he caught his reflection in the mirror behind the bar and it saddened him even more. His once handsome appearance had aged dramatically the last few years. His jowls hung loosely from the sides of his face, and the dark circles under his heavily wrinkled eyes were now permanent features. His hair, once full and black, now covered only the sides of his head like dirty snowfall and looked more like overcooked pasta than anything else. The thirty or so extra pounds that spread over his belt were more from his ulcer and digestive problems than from a hearty appetite. He drank more than he slept and he slept more than he smiled. All and all, he concluded his life was a mess and only getting worse.

Refilling his glass, he returned to his desk and stared blankly at the walls of his private study. Beautifully lacquered photographs of his many personal accomplishments and political highlights surrounded the room. On the wall directly behind him hung a half dozen portraits of him shaking the hands of various United States Presidents. To the left, he posed with ten or twelve of the most influential men and women in the world. To his right, behind the wet bar, his family in their varied stages of life smiled back at him. For so many years he had looked upon these walls as a source of great pride, but now they only seemed to mock him.

The knock on his study door startled him momentarily, but he quickly regained his composure as his wife entered the room.

"Bob," Gloria Allsworth said as she stepped meekly toward her husband's desk. "I hate to disturb you but I really do need your advice."

"What is it now Gloria," the Senator said with no effort to hide his annoyance.

"Well," Gloria began, dismissing her husband's curt response. " I was just finishing up the seating arrangements for Allison and Adam's engagement party next week, and to my horror, I realized I sat Judge Blackman and his wife next to Congressman Wilkes and his wife. Do you think there's still bad blood between them or should I just leave it be?" she asked with great concern.

The Senator continued staring at the walls of his study as though in deep thought over the dilemma. Finally, turning to his wife he asked innocently, "Blackman and Wilkes don't get along?"

"Oh Bob, really!" Gloria said with exaggerated disbelief. "How you can be so insensitive is beyond me. Don't you remember six months ago when Margaret Wilkes had that fundraiser for her husband and neglected to invite the Judge and his wife? My God, it was the talk of the bridge club for weeks."

The Senator sighed heavily and rubbed his eyes for a long moment before speaking. "Gloria, I'm sure in the minds of your bridge club, that was an unforgivable slight, but I assure you, in the real world, neither the Judge nor his wife were the least bit offended. They are Republicans, after all."

"Bob, I don't think…"

"Gloria, please," he replied curtly. "I really do have quite a bit of work to finish this morning. I'll leave the seating arrangements to your discretion. Please ask Charles to see to it I am not disturbed for the next couple of hours."

Although he phrased his words carefully, Gloria knew her husband well enough to know it was more of an order than a request.

"Very well dear. I'll take care of the guest list myself," she said indignantly. "But don't say I didn't warn you."

After the door closed behind her, the Senator reached for the phone and dialed the home number of his attorney and long-time friend. A few moments later, he was speaking to Neil MacGregor.

"Good morning Senator," Mac began with his usual easy-going manner. "Must be a free breakfast going on somewhere to get you up this early on a Monday. What can I do for you?"

"Mac, I need to meet with you. It's urgent," the Senator said quickly.

"Today Bob? Can't it wait till Wednesday? I'm really tied up with…"

"Today Mac, please. It has to be today."

"All right, Bob. Today it is then. How about one o'clock at the club," Mac said, noting with concern the panic in his friend's voice.

"Fine. I'll see you at one."

"STOP, STOP, STOP!" hollered Allison Allsworth. "The lightings all wrong!"

For the eighth time in the past two hours, she again ordered the lights redirected, the set changed, her make-up retouched and hair redone.

"For the love of God Marcy, from what agency did these so-called professionals come from? Did you even bother to check their references?" Allison ranted after a delicate sip of Perrier water.

Marcy quickly scurried over to her boss with a fresh bottle of water and frantically flipped through pages on her clipboard. "Mr. and Mrs. Alfred Hutchins both said they were very pleased with the way their daughter's engagement picture turned out, Ms. Allsworth," Marcy answered submissively.

"Oh please, Marcy," Allison responded with her usual disdain. "The mere fact that the lens didn't crack during little Angela's photo shoot was enough of a surprise for the Hutchins' family. I can't believe you booked the same photographer as that stuck-up little bitch. What *were* you thinking?"

"I'm...I'm sorry, Ms. Allsworth. Let me go talk to them and try to explain exactly what it is you're looking for them to do."

"You do that Marcy. And make sure they understand exactly who they are photographing."

Allison watched her aide quickly depart. Why did everything happen to her, she thought. On what should be one of her happiest days, everything was going wrong. Her mother's neurotic obsession with the seating arrangements, her younger sister's insistence on not only screwing up her own life, but dragging down the family name as well, and her father's lackluster performance in the latest polls were all taking their toll. The truth was Allison was used to the first two, but was having great difficulty adjusting to the possibility she would no longer be the eldest daughter of a very powerful Senator.

After forty years in the United States Senate, Allison knew her father's political existence was on life support. She knew her elite status would suffer terribly if she were just the daughter of a rich family. There were plenty of rich families in Massachusetts, but only two that could claim a seat in the Senate.

How could her father do this to her? Why now, when she was so close to starting her own political legacy did he have to lose an election? She had seen the change in her father more than two years ago. It was then she knew she had to secure a future of her own. And it was then she met Adam MacGregor. She knew immediately, *he* had what it took to keep her in the lifestyle she had grown accustomed. Soon she would marry into one of the richest families in the state, and with her guidance, be the wife of one of the most successful politicians in history.

"Excuse me Ms. Allsworth," Marcy interrupted meekly. "I've rewritten your wedding announcement and I think I have it right this time."

"It had better be right, Marcy. I can't imagine you screwing it up again," Allison said harshly, taking the notice from Marcy's hand. After checking it thoroughly, she sighed and handed it back to the aide. "This will be fine Marcy. Only four attempts to write a five-line paragraph. How *has* the literary world survived all these years without you?"

The moment Paige Allsworth entered the Pine Street Inn, a homeless shelter in downtown Boston, she knew her day would only get worse. An optimistic person by nature, she was feeling an unusual sense of dread and foreboding since early morning. No matter how many times she tried to shake the feeling loose, it clung to her like static electricity.

"Good morning, Ms. Allsworth," one of the janitors said as she passed by the front desk.

"Hello Tom. How are you this morning?" she asked with a feigned pleasantness.

"Just fine Ms. Allsworth. Just fine. Did you hear the weatherman's calling for snow later today?" he asked as he continued mopping the front entrance.

Great, she thought, not stopping to continue the conversation.

The hallways were scattered with homeless men, women, and children all varying in age and degrees of helplessness. Some of the faces were familiar, but many were not.

After three years as a social worker, Paige still couldn't get use to the sight of so many displaced, forgotten citizens. Growing up the youngest daughter of a U.S. Senator, she knew she had been isolated from the poverty and suffering of others. She just had no idea how isolated.

As a senior at Emerson College, she had decided to do her social thesis on the homeless situation in Boston and naturally choose the Inn as her focal point. Lauren Woodard, the Inn's administrator, introduced her to the shocking reality of life on the streets. For close to three hours, she passionately described to Paige a world of single mothers, abandoned children, forgotten veterans, and discarded humanity.

Three weeks later, her eyes wide open and the truth hammering away at her beliefs, Paige returned to the Inn as a volunteer. Upon graduating, she took a full-time position as one of three social workers at the Inn. As was to be expected, her parents were shocked and disappointed with her decision and even begged her not to embarrass them with such a choice of careers.

If there were one phrase which summed up her adolescent years, "please don't embarrass the family," would be it. It seemed to her everything she did, everything she tried, and everything she said, in some way embarrassed a member of her family.

God knew it wasn't intentional. She wanted nothing more than to be like her older sister, but the harder she tried the more she failed. Unlike Allison, Paige was not one to ignore right from wrong just to keep the peace.

Once, at the age of twelve, she was sent home from an all-girl Catholic school for refusing to participate in the live dissection of a frog. She tried explaining to her father the experiment was cruel and unnecessary, but received the usual curt response halfway through her explanation.

"I've heard enough young lady," her father said through clenched teeth. "Go to your room while your mother and I discuss a suitable punishment."

Later that evening, after her father had been drinking, she overheard an argument that would forever haunt her.

"I told you thirteen years ago not to go through with the pregnancy. I only wanted Allison. Only one child, but no, you weren't satisfied with that, were you?" her father slurred angrily.

"Keep your voice down, Bob. She'll hear you. I didn't plan to get pregnant. You know that. If I had gotten an abortion like you wanted the press would have crucified you in the next election. Paige may not be as polished as Allison, but at least she's not making headlines like Congressman Jackson's son. I'm sure she'll outgrow this stage sooner or later and until then we'll just have to try to keep her antics private."

Not only an embarrassment, but also an unplanned, unwanted one at that.

Upon graduation, the tension between father and daughter grew unchecked until Paige finally moved from the mansion in Hyannisport to a small apartment in Cambridge. That was two years ago and the situation was yet to improve.

Finally arriving at her cramped, cluttered office, Paige arranged herself behind her equally cramped and cluttered desk. She took a deep breath and tried coming to terms with the depressed feelings which engulfed her upon waking. It took her all of five seconds to put her finger on the source of her foul mood. It was the party this weekend at her parent's house to announce the engagement of her sister to Adam MacGregor.

It wasn't the party so much that bothered her or the fact she'd have to spend the weekend at the mansion. Though neither would have been on her top one hundred preferred activities for any weekend. Rather it was the guest of honor.

Adam MacGregor.

The man she had been in love with since they first met more than two years ago at a fund-raiser for her father. Allison didn't even know he existed until Paige made the mistake of mentioning how attracted she was to him.

After that, she never stood a chance.

Like some medieval sorceress conjuring an ancient spell, Allison enthralled, enchanted, and seduced Adam with her infinite charm. At first, it was like a game to Allison, a simple and easy way to spite her younger sister. However, once she learned who Adam was, and the potential he possessed, the stakes were raised considerably. With unabashed determination Allison flirted, tempted and lured Adam into her intricately braided web like a black widow spider toying with an unsuspecting housefly.

For the past two and a half years, Paige's only consolation was the fact her and Adam had become the best of friends. They could talk for hours about anything from politics to religion, from this year's fall fashions to last year's fall classic, to whether Bill Russell was the best center ever to grace the NBA to whether Mozart's operas were the best to ever grace the stage.

There were so many more things though she wished to do with him, so many more things she wished to share. Little things like how much she loved him and what a mistake it would be to marry Allison.

It was bad enough she had to spend the weekend at her parents, but unbearable to be there to celebrate the engagement of her sister to the man she loved. With any luck, the expected snowfall would develop into a weeklong blizzard stranding her in Cambridge and forcing her to miss the blessed occasion. More than likely though, she would be present and in typical Allsworth fashion lie through her teeth about how happy she was for them both.

CHAPTER *Three*

"Congratulations, son," Mac beamed as Adam stepped off the elevator onto the twelfth floor office suite. "I've had my secretary buy every copy of the morning paper in three counties. We're all so very proud of you!"

Neil MacGregor's oversized frame stood squarely in front of the receptionist's desk. With one arm draped over Adam's shoulder, he enthusiastically shook his son's hand. The receptionist, a group of paralegals, and a couple of passing attorneys also applauded Mac's statement before returning to their daily grind. Adam blushed and tried to appear as humble and nonchalant about his achievement as the circumstances permitted. He'd already received confirmation from the Board of Bar Overseers concerning his recent bar exam and knew his father would make a bigger deal than was necessary.

"What happened to your hand?" Mac suddenly asked, noting the white gauze hiding all but the fingers.

"Oh, I cut it slicing a bagel," Adam lied. "Never attempt to use a sharp knife before your first cup of coffee," he added from his rehearsed answer.

Mac smiled and congratulated his son again as they proceeded to the thirteenth floor. "It's really not that big of a deal, Mac," Adam said as they exited the elevator. "Seventy-eight others passed the same exam."

"Maybe so, son, but did any of the others graduate first in their class from Yale, or become the youngest editor of the Law Review in their universities' history, or receive sixteen job offers from the biggest law firms from New York to California? I'll give you your first piece of advice as an attorney son, 'Stop being so modest,'" Mac finished with a hearty laugh.

As they continued toward Mac's corner office, his co-workers greeted Adam with congratulations while Mac was stopped a dozen times or so to sign one document or another. All tolled MacGregor and Associates employed eighty-two attorneys and had a support staff in excess of two hundred. Since leaving the District Attorney's office over twenty-five years ago, Mac had built one of the largest and most successful law practices in the country.

"I suppose I'm going to have to give you a raise now," Mac said as they settled into his private office.

Adam grinned uncomfortably in the leather armchair. "Mac, I need a raise like you need more clients. Let's just keep our financial arrangement the way it is, please. I owe you more than any amount of money could ever repay," Adam said sincerely.

"Well son, you're a tough negotiator. But you learned from the best. Actually, it wasn't so much a monetary raise I had in mind," Mac answered while opening a cardboard box next to his desk.

Though he was fifty-seven years old and his thick black hair was now peppered with more than a hint of gray, Adam couldn't help noticing the child-like excitement in his father's face. Mac removed several sheets of letterhead from the box and handed them over the desk toward Adam. Across the top of the page it read **MacGregor and Son Law Firm.** Adam stared in amazement at the paper for several seconds before looking back toward his father.

"Mac, I...I don't know what to say." The lump forming in his throat made it difficult to say even that.

"There's no need to say anything son," Mac said, coming around the desk to look Adam square in the eyes. "You've brought me more joy and happiness than I could have ever hoped for. The circumstances that brought us together couldn't have been more tragic, but never once did

I ever regret my decision. I couldn't love you or be more proud of you if you were my own biological son."

The two men hugged for several seconds, hoping the other didn't notice the tear in their eye or the shakiness in the voice.

"I love you too, dad," Adam finally said as the embrace ended.

"Well," Mac said steadying himself, "this is shaping up to be quite a week for you, isn't it son? This morning you officially entered the ranks of the legal profession, a couple of hours later you make partner, and this weekend Senator Allsworth and his wife are hosting a party in honor of you engagement to Allison."

Adam's expression changed dramatically as he turned from Mac and walked pensively toward the windows near the front of the office. The troubled expression didn't escape Mac though.

"Son, are you all right?" he asked bluntly.

Adam took a moment to compose himself and managed his best smile before answering. "I'm fine, Mac. Just a little tired that's all."

"Come on Adam. You might be able to fool a jury with that look, but not your old man. You're having those nightmares again, aren't you?"

"Mac, please don't start. I'm fine really. I've just been under a lot of pressure lately, with the engagement coming up and studying for the bar. It's nothing, honest."

Mac nodded toward his son thoughtfully, not sure whether to believe him or not, but finally giving in to the excuse. "Very well, Adam. How about you and I check out your new office. There's a new pro bono case we received Friday and I'd like you to take a look at it."

Adam's new office was somewhat more boastful than the small cubicle he'd worked from the last three summers and yet it avoided the cumbersome look favored by many of his contemporaries.

He had to hand it to Mac, or more likely his secretary, they had done a first rate job decorating. A large handcrafted oak desk and several leather armchairs were centered near the rear of the office and several large ferns rested squarely on the plush beige carpet. A floor-to-ceiling mahogany bookcase ran the length of one wall and housed an impressive collection of law books. Behind his desk hung his college diploma and law school degree, a picture of he and Mac on a fishing trip they took two years earlier and a picture of him and three law school buddies skiing last year in Aspen. On the desk was a picture of his fiancée Allison Allsworth in a white evening gown and displaying enough jewelry to finance the purchase of a third world country.

Two years ago when they first met, Adam was convinced she was the most beautiful and interesting person alive. He thought he had found his soul mate, his one true love.

That was two years ago though and now he wasn't so sure.

As he glared back at the photograph, he struggled with the internal debate that seemed to occupy most of his waking hours. Was he making a mistake marrying the daughter of one of the most influential and powerful men in the United States? A woman who possessed every quality a man could desire including beauty, wealth, intelligence, and passion? Was he ready to make such an enormous commitment, both emotionally and financially? More to the point, was he marrying the *wrong sister?*

There was no defining moment in his and Allison's relationship that he could point to as the beginning of the end. Instead, it had been a gradual awareness that Allison's beauty was indeed only skin deep. An awareness that she had goals and aspirations far different and remote from anything he wished to attain in life. He was sure Allison would be just as happy with any man with two middle names, a Roman numeral at the end and a substantial trust fund in the bank.

Just as gradual as his wilting affection for Allison was his growing attraction to Paige. His awareness that certain emotions were creeping ever so slowly beyond that of friendship and bordering on true feelings of love. Everyday, for more than two years, their friendship had inched that much closer to something special, something wonderful and full of promise. And it was because of these feelings he knew in his heart he would have to break off his engagement to Allison.

Regardless of the pain and humiliation both families would suffer and regardless of what it meant in terms of his professional future, marrying Allison Allsworth was definitely a mistake.

HE IS COMING!

The words suddenly flashed through his mind. All morning he tried to put the strange events in his bedroom to rest. He was sure the stress of studying for the bar and the inevitable break-up with Allison had been the cause of the nightmares and that morning's bizarre phenomenon.

HE IS COMING!

Sitting on the corner of his desk, a slight throbbing taking life behind his left eye, Adam stared at his injured right hand. How was it possible to blackout for twenty-eight minutes, yet retrieve a kitchen knife, change into an outfit from Beach Blanket Bingo, cut his hand deep enough to draw blood, and write such a strange message without remembering any of it?

HE IS COMING!

Who or what was coming and when? Perhaps the event was some residue from the elusive nightmare hours before or from some horror movie he'd seen years earlier. He was sure there had to be a rational, sane explanation for his behavior. Some documented medical term for a once-in-a-lifetime slip from reality.

Still, Adam found himself flipping through the yellow pages until he found the number of Doctor Matthew Jellison, Mac's longtime physician. After making small talk with the nurse, Adam was able to secure a four o'clock appointment for that day due to an earlier cancellation. He thanked the nurse and quickly hung up.

Adam tried to ignore the growing pain in his temples by studying the pro bono case Mac had given him earlier. Though the firm dealt mainly with corporate law, the courts did assign the office a criminal case from time to time. And as was the practice, the new guy, whether a newly made partner or not, received the dubious distinction of handling the case. He opened the file and read through the state's case against Mr. David Green, alias David White, alias David Black.

Colorful defendant, Adam thought.

According to the state, Mr. Green was the proprietor of the Love Hole, a strip club in Boston's Red Light district and the owner of a rap sheet as long as Adam's arm. Over the course of the last three years, Mr. Green had been arrested for various offences ranging from drug possession to illegal arms sale.

On the night in question, Mr. Green was stopped on a routine traffic violation and after a subsequent search of his vehicle was booked for unlawful possession of firearms and possession of false identification for the purpose of fraud. Mr. Green was presently a resident of the Charles Street Jail pending his arraignment later that afternoon.

Adam closed the file and called the administrative office of the prison. After introducing himself, he made an appointment to meet with his new client at one-thirty that afternoon.

Under normal circumstances, he would been have thrilled with the prospect of his first attorney-client interview, but the experiences of the past few days had been anything but normal. No longer even able to go through the motions of reading Mr. Green's case more closely, Adam rose from his desk and walked toward the window. Thirteen floors above the financial district of Boston, he stared aimlessly out at South Station and the hustling crowds below.

Lost in his thoughts, he never noticed the telescope set up directly across from his office nor the man watching him in the adjacent building.

CHAPTER *Four*

The room smelled of disinfectant and the white walls glistened from the reflection of high-magnitude fluorescent lighting. The low rumble of the machine beside Alec resonated quietly throughout his body, and the peaceful intonation of classical music played softly through his headphones. With the virtual reality goggles strapped tightly to his head, Alec watched repeatedly the selected programming of the Organization's desired sequence of events.

Doctor Josef Wenzler sat with two technicians on the opposite side of a one way mirror. They watched intently as Alec continued to undergo subconscious conditioning for his next mission. While the technicians busied themselves with the subliminal messages hidden throughout the music, Wenzler continued to study the progress.

"Track change into bluegrass," one technician said.

"Ready," the other replied while adjusting the knobs.

A nurse appeared in the room with Alec and stared at her reflection in the mirror, awaiting her signal. As the classical ensemble gave way to the more upbeat tempo of the bluegrass instruments, Alec involuntarily jerked to the left. The lights dimmed momentarily and the nurse nodded toward her reflection. Picking up one of the three syringes on the table to her left, she proceeded to inject it into the left arm of Alec.

"Fifteen minutes until the next injection," the technician closest to Wenzler said softly into the intercom.

Wenzler leaned forward, almost touching the glass with his nose, as he studied Alec for any signs of an adverse reaction. Satisfied with the result, he leaned back and scribbled a notation on his chart.

"Increase the dosage by fifteen millimeters, Mr. Morris," he said calmly.

The two technicians glanced at one another apprehensively, then at Doctor Wenzler.

"*Fifteen* millimeters, sir?" Morris asked hesitantly.

The doctor slowly took his eyes from the chart and stared deliberately at the technician.

At seventy-four years of age, Wenzler's physical appearance was misleading. With a thick shock of white hair, aged but smooth skin, and bushy eyebrows like caterpillars, he appeared as nothing more than a harmless, good-natured grandfather. However, to those who knew him, Doctor Wenzler was anything but a harmless, good-natured grandfather. He possessed a meanness that flowed through him like water through a sieve. Rumors had him linked with everything from a Nazi concentration camp to a special interrogator for a certain South American dictator.

"That's what I said, Mr. Morris. Do you have a problem following that order?"

"No sir. It's just that…well, it's just that Alec's never been exposed to those levels before and…"

Wenzler slammed the chart down violently and rose quickly from his seat. With two quick strides he was nose to nose with the technician.

"When it becomes necessary for a technician to question my judgement, Mr. Morris, I shall recommend you. Until that time though you shall carry out my orders without comment or suggestion. Is that understood!"

Wenzler's ruddy complexion glowed and his steel gray eyes held the subordinate speechless and terrified. There was no one in the Organization more dangerous to cross than the good doctor.

"I'm...I'm sorry sir. Please forgive my insolence. I spoke out of line," the technician groveled.

Wenzler continued his icy stare for several moments, taking great pleasure in watching the technician squirm. Finally he broke the stare and turned back toward Alec.

"Increase the dosage, Mr. Morris," he said calmly as though the confrontation never happened.

Easing himself back into the chair, Wenzler continued to stare at his subject. Something was wrong with Alec, something very wrong, and Wenzler was feeling the pressure.

As head of the Organization's Scientific Research Center it was his responsibility to determine the cause and correct it immediately. However after almost three months, he was no closer to a cause, never mind a cure. They had tried everything from antibiotic steroids to genetically enhanced vitamins to an influx of white corpuscles to replace those lost during teleportation, but so far all had failed.

There was no way the Organization could contain the rage and anger Alec displayed when he wasn't sedated. Even while in hypnotic somnolence, Alec thrashed about violently, kicking and fighting some imaginary demon.

Wenzler knew Alec's failure to perform would be seen as his failure to perform as well. But more importantly, Alec's degree of usefulness to the Organization would be measured against his own degree of usefulness to the Organization. As it was, Omega had been pushing for the doctor to step down for several years and this was exactly what he needed to succeed. Wenzler knew he couldn't allow Alec's problem to continue unresolved for much longer.

The Keisler Institute for Genetic Research was located in an eight-story office building overlooking the Charles River. Its occupants were phony corporations staffed by the Organization and were used as one of its many fronts.

Omega inserted his access card into the side entrance, made an obligatory nod toward the armed guard behind the desk, and took the stairs to the second floor. Pulling open one of the glass doors which led into the small waiting area of the Institute, he continued past the receptionist and went directly to the offices of Genetic Technologies, Inc.

Using a second access card and a nine digit code, he proceeded into the bare, unlit office. The lights automatically engaged when he crossed the threshold, as did the three surveillance cameras mounted invisibly into the ceiling. The elevator on the back wall was not hidden or disguised. If an intruder had made it this far, then surely they knew what they were looking for and why.

Engaging the security doors, first with his thumbprint, then with an optical scan, the elevator door slid quietly open. A moment later, Omega exited into the sub-basement of the Organizations nervous system. His patent leather shoes echoed loudly off the gray concrete walls and similar flooring until he reached the Satellite Surveillance and Monitoring Station. He entered the facility, passing the eighty or so technicians it took to run the operation, pausing briefly outside the Scientific Research room.

Peering through the small slit in one of the lead-plated iron doors, Omega watched the two men dressed in white radioactive suits. They stood on either side of a nine-year-old boy with sandy blonde hair and pale blue eyes. The child wore only a pair of green gym shorts and a green T-shirt. An infectious smile danced across his lips when he noticed Omega staring through the window. The two men also noticed Omega, but his attention was on the small boy known only as number six. He smiled at the child, then noted the gauge on the outside door indicating a radiation level currently five times greater than the average human body could tolerate.

Satisfied with what he saw, he waved to the child and continued onto the sanctuary of his office. Sitting behind the computer terminal, he entered his password and waited while the computer confirmed his identity.

"Welcome Omega," the computer voice finally answered.

"Good morning computer," Omega politely replied. "I'd like to review the Judgement Day files, please," he instructed the voice-operated computer program.

Within seconds the screen appeared before him. With the aid of the program in front of him, Omega could access every police report, court decision, and jury finding in the United States and Puerto Rico. The program had been modified to narrow the list considerably. Omega and the Organization were only interested in cases where the defendants had been set free due to quirks in the legal system such as loopholes, procedural errors, lenient judges, or bleeding-heart juries.

Those cases in which the evidence was so overwhelming, that a trial was a forgone conclusion. Cases which the legal systems overzealous concern with the rights of the accused had foreshadowed the rights of the victim and that of justice. Only cases in which the Organization was required to right such an obvious wrong.

While the computer went on-line checking through tens of thousands of criminal cases, Omega sat back with an updated printout of last month's report. Of the forty-two names originally listed, thirty-nine had been eliminated through various intervening acts of the Organization. Justice was scheduled for the remaining three later that day.

Jesse Diego was a three-time loser from Detroit, Michigan. With a rap sheet starting around his ninth birthday, Mr. Diego had found himself in and out of juvenile detention centers and state prisons for the past nineteen years.

Five months ago, he was arrested and charged with raping a thirteen-year-old runaway. His lawyer, an overzealous public defendant, argued Mr. Diego's constitutional rights were violated when the arresting officers failed to read him his Miranda rights and procured a confession without allowing Mr. Diego time to contact his attorney. The thirteen-year-old runaway disappeared and the judge had no choice but to dismiss the case. When the Organization's field team arrived in his Detroit neighborhood later today, having his Miranda's read to him will be the least of Mr. Diego's concerns.

John Caleb was a thirty-nine year old unemployed carpenter from Jacksonville, Florida. Two years ago, Drug Enforcement Agents broke down the door to his motel room and confiscated fifteen kilos of cocaine. However, Florida's State Board of Appeals overturned the easy conviction because of a typographical error on the search warrant. Instead of room 12, the secretary inadvertently typed room 21. As a result, John Caleb was a free man. At some point today though, John Caleb would be a dead man. Omega carefully drew a line through the names of both men.

However, it was the third name on the list that concerned Omega. He wished more than anything he could cross out the name of Eduard Santiago. The Colombian drug lord was well connected and well protected. It would be suicide to send in a field team. The only chance the Organization had at eliminating Santiago cleanly was by using Alec. And that was reason for concern.

There was a quick rap on his door and William Jennings entered.

"Hope you don't mind the intrusion, sir," Jennings said respectively. "I just thought you'd like to know Jesse Diego was killed this morning in an apparent drug deal gone bad. Initial reports from Detroit intelligence confirm no witnesses, no clues, and not much attention. The field team's on their way back now," he added proudly, as if he were the one responsible for the clean hit.

Omega smiled and darkened the line across Diego's name.

"And Caleb? Any news yet?"

"No sir, nothing yet. I'll let you know though as soon as the team reports in," Jennings said quickly.

"Is Alec on schedule?" Omega asked casually, trying not to show his concern.

"Doctor Wenzler's with him now. He's implanting the ninety second recall and going over some last minute details," Jennings answered. "Would you like me to get you an update?"

"No Jennings, thank you but that won't be necessary. Please keep me informed though on the Jacksonville field team's progress."

The man tipped his head slightly and bowed out of the office. Omega sat for several seconds staring at the name of Eduard Santiago. "Pull yourself together for this one Alec. You may not be getting another chance."

Chapter *Five*

His objective was the second floor master bedroom, but as his vision focused and his head cleared, Alec realized he had once again missed his destination. He was standing in the lower foyer, alone, but surely not for long. His target was wealthy and well protected. Eduard Santiago had ignored the warnings of the Organization and continued his deluge of illegal drug trafficking into the United States. Now it was up to Alec to put an end to Eduard Santiago.

He checked the stopwatch on his left wrist and noted approximately ninety seconds before recall. The AK-47 semi-automatic Uzi in his right hand was fully loaded and capable of up to a hundred and fifty rounds if things got complicated. Alec could only hope things would get complicated.

He needed to kill as desperately as a thirsty man needed to drink or a starving man needed to eat. The rage inside him was building. Slowly but surely, it was building.

The house was dark with the exception of a single light emanating from what he knew to be the kitchen. Several voices, all speaking in Spanish, flowed from the room. Alec was fluent in fifteen languages and knew from the conversation that they were too preoccupied with their card game to have noticed his arrival.

With gentle, gazelle-like movements, he swiftly mounted the spiral staircase, pausing briefly to orientate himself in the hallway. The Organization intended for him to teleport directly into the master bedroom, but they had taken precautions against a misfire by famil-iarizing him with blueprints of the Santiago's fortress.

As with his previous four missions, the unexplained rage eating away at him like a cancer had limited his ability to concentrate.

In the past, he had successfully eliminated over a hundred men and women who stood in the way of the Organization's goal. However, over the past three months there had been a significant drop in his efficiency.

The nightmares, headaches, and his inability to teleport accurately had raised doubts in the minds of the Organization. They were reluc-tant to send him out on more than two missions per month and recently implanted a mandatory recall into his subconscious mind in the event of his capture or death.

Precautions which only heightened his rage.

He was confident though that this particular mission would put to rest their doubts.

The bedroom was to the left, three doors down. He was calm and objective. His heartbeat ticked in sync with his wristwatch, which showed only fifty-eight seconds till recall. At the bedroom door, he heard the soft breathing of at least two people. Glancing up and down the hall-way one last time, he entered Santiago's lair with great anticipation.

A man and a woman, both naked, lay sprawled across each other in a grotesque configuration. He could feel his heart rate increase, as the thought of their deaths became imminent.

He crept slowly to the woman's side of the bed first even though she was not his intended mark. Her dark-skinned nakedness was arousing, sensual, and forbidden, but he was drawn to it nevertheless. He fought the need to reach down and touch her, run his hands over her small supple breasts, press his lips against hers, but she was tainted.

She had slept with the enemy.

He forced himself to look away, to cast his eyes upon Santiago, the man he was here to kill. Crossing to the other side of the bed, he took a deep breath and cocked the semi-automatic with a sense of fulfillment.

He nudged the man with the Uzi, waiting for him to awake. He wanted the pleasure of seeing the look of fear in Santiago's eyes before taking his pathetic life.

The man was slow to wake though, mumbling and trying to turn onto his side, before finally opening his eyes.

"Good morning, Eduard," was the last thing his victim heard before his skull exploded with the force of the Uzi.

The woman woke, startled, and covered with blood and fragments of what use to be Santiago's head.

"I'm sorry to have disturbed you bitch. Please, go back to sleep." Alec smiled broadly before sending her to the same fate as the scum lying dead next to her.

From downstairs, he heard the hurried steps of the guards rushing toward the bedroom just as his stopwatch beeped its five-second warning. He wished he had more time. Time to empty the remaining magazine in his Uzi. Time to satisfy the rage that still burned inside him.

But his body began to tingle and felt slightly numb as the recall was set in motion. Moments before the guards burst into the bedroom, he vanished.

The bullets sprayed randomly, some digging deep into the white walls, others shattering light fixtures and assorted equipment. Bottles of drugs, serums, tablets, capsules, and powdered ingredients needed to compound more exotic medicines crashed to the floor. Wenzler watched in horror as Alec spun around, his finger tightly clenching the trigger, looking for someone or something to damage.

From behind the bulletproof wall, Wenzler prayed Alec's rage would blind him to the five guards laying face down on the concrete floor only a foot or two away.

When the last of the hundred and fifty rounds were expelled, the guards, two with tranquilizer guns and one with a straight jacket, positioned themselves in an attempt to restrain Alec. The first guard was killed instantly when Alec thrust forward with his open palm and splintered the bone in the man's nose, pushing it through his brain.

"Shit!" Wenzler cursed loudly.

A second guard managed to shoot Alec in the upper back with a high-powered tranquilizer dart, but before it could slow him down, Alec swung his right leg around in a sweeping high arc, catching the man's chin. The force of the kick snapped his neck, and he too died instantly.

Two more darts penetrated Alec's flesh before he stumbled forward and fell to his knees.

The remaining men quickly restrained him with the straight jacket and forced him to the ground.

"KILL HIM! I... MUST ... KILL... HIM," Alec forced the words as he struggled with consciousness.

Once restrained, Wenzler quickly entered the lab and motioned for the remaining guards to leave. Removing a syringe from his white lab coat, he injected Alec's right arm slowly.

"Can you hear me, Alec?" Wenzler asked in a slow, deliberate tone.

Alec looked up; his face contorted with anger and hate, but said nothing.

"You must listen to me, Alec. You must understand. He *is* dead. Do you understand me? He *is* dead."

Alec only struggled harder against the restraints. His teeth clenched and eyes bulging, he repeated his earlier threat.

"MUST KILL HIM. NOT... LIKE... ME! Must kill... before...."

The words trailed off into a raspy growl before Alec submitted to the effect of the drugs. Signaling for the technicians to re-enter the room, Wenzler removed a second syringe and injected Alec's left arm.

"Take him to the neurological lab and prep him for a CAT scan and full brain wave alteration. Keep him heavily sedated. I don't want him waking up." Wenzler ordered.

As the technicians wheeled Alec out of the room, Wenzler stood alone, shaking his head.

"Where have I failed you, Alec? Where have we failed each other?" he said to the empty room.

✶✶✶✶✶✶✶✶✶✶✶✶✶✶✶✶✶✶✶✶✶✶✶✶✶✶✶✶✶✶✶✶✶

CHAPTER *Six*

"Pastrami on rye please," Adam said to the man behind the deli, "extra mustard and a small coke."

He finished the legal brief shortly after one o'clock, but was told Mac had left on an unscheduled appointment with the Senator, and so Adam went to lunch alone. He wasn't the least bit disappointed and had actually been relieved when Mac's secretary said he wouldn't be returning for at least another hour.

The headache, which began slowly in the back of his head, steadily worked its way through the rest of his skull. He walked the couple of blocks to Lenny's Deli, hoping the brisk air would at least offer a reprieve from the pain. By the time he reached Faniuel Hall, a trendy food court and shopping area downtown, he was pleased to find his self-prescribed medication worked. The pain had at least diminished to a dull ache.

He paid for his lunch and headed to the back of the deli carrying his briefcase in one hand and balancing a tray in the other. The first flakes of snow had gently begun to drift aimlessly to the ground, disappearing almost on contact with the cobblestones that lined the street.

Three to four inches was what the weatherman was forecasting.

Without realizing it, he began worrying about Paige driving in the pending snowstorm. She had insisted on taking him to dinner tonight in honor of his official entrance into the legal profession, but now Adam wondered if he should call and suggest they wait until tomorrow evening or perhaps offer to pick her up at work. It would be an innocent enough offer. After all, everyone, including Allison, knew they were close friends.

A lead ball settled uneasily in the pit of his stomach as he realized that to Paige they probably were *just* friends.

The truth was, even though he was falling in love with Paige, he was not looking forward to seeing her. He was afraid his true feelings were becoming as transparent as the window in front of him. Soon someone would notice the admiring glances he gave her or the unusual amount of attention he paid to her every word or the way he laughed and smiled and acted like a schoolboy whenever she was near. Lately, trying to hide his feelings from her was like trying to hide a fire in the dark.

Taking a bite of his sandwich, he glanced up at the other patrons in the deli. The tourists had all disappeared with the changing of the seasons and only true Bostonians, most also on lunch break, filled the seats. Three well-dressed men Adam recognized from court sat at a corner booth. The one on the end was telling a story that seemed to amuse the other two. An older gentleman with white hair covered by a tweed fedora sat alone at the counter. And a man with dark sunglasses, wearing a Celtics cap and a green Celtics jacket was smoking a cigarette three tables in front of him. He directed his gaze out onto the cobblestone walkway, where the light snowfall continued its lazy decent. Taking another bite from his sandwich, he washed it down with a sip of soda and weighed the pros and cons of canceling his dinner date.

"Excuse me," said the man with the tweed fedora. A sheepish grin played across his face, "Aren't you Adam MacGregor?" Caught off guard, Adam instinctively stood to shake the man's hand.

"Yes," he answered, "I am. I'm sorry, have we met?"

The man firmly shook Adam's hand and said, "My name is Peter Jones. You went to undergraduate school with my son, Patrick. We met briefly at the graduation ceremonies."

Adam took a moment to run the name through his memory, vaguely recalling a Patrick Jones.

"Yes, of course," he answered as casually as he could. "How is Patrick?"

"Wonderful, just wonderful. He works only a couple of blocks from here as a stockbroker for Dean Whittier. I was suppose to meet him for lunch, but he had to cancel at the last minute. A problem with a client's portfolio or something like that. Do you mind if I join you?" he asked, the sheepish grin still spread broadly across his face.

"Of course not, Mr. Jones. Please," Adam said, holding his arm out toward an empty chair.

"Thank you, Adam. Boy, now Patrick will be doubly disappointed he couldn't get away."

As the man pulled out the chair, Adam noticed for the first time the left sleeve of his jacket was pinned to his side. Catching the glimpse, Jones casually nodded to the missing arm and said nonchalantly, "Vietnam, sixty-five. A buddy of mine, a few feet in front of me, stepped on a land mine. We never knew what hit us. I woke up in an army hospital two weeks later, missing an arm and wearing the Purple Heart. Four days later I received an honorable discharge."

"I'm sorry, Mr. Jones, I didn't mean to stare," Adam said embarrassed.

"Don't be. My buddy wasn't so lucky. Besides, I've had almost thirty years to accept it. It's quite useful really. I'm always offered a seat on the subway, and I get the best parking places at the malls," he said with a smile.

An awkward silence hung thickly between them as the two men fidgeted in their seats. Adam felt like a schoolboy sitting in the principal's office awaiting a stern reprimand.

"So tell me Adam, what's new in your life?" Jones finally asked. "I'm sure Patrick's going to want to know."

Where to begin, Adam thought. *Today I made partner in one of the largest law firms on the East Coast. Later this week I'm supposed to announce my engagement to the daughter of the state's senior Senator. But of course I'm going to break it off because I'm really in love with her younger sister. And let's not forget the terrible headaches and nightmares that keep me up all hours of the night. More recently, just this morning as a matter of fact, I blacked out for almost a half-hour while dressing in a really bad outfit and nearly cut off my fingers.*

"Well I'm afraid it's the same old grind day in and day out for me, Mr. Jones. I'm working for my father's law firm a block or two from here. Other than that, not much at all is happening in my life," Adam said, deciding not to burden the man with his troubles.

"You're young, Adam. Things aren't always as they seem," Jones said with certain sadness in his eyes.

Adam couldn't be sure, but he had the distinct feeling that there was more on the man's mind than just the small talk transpiring between them. Though he couldn't put his finger on it, something about the man seemed familiar. It was more than just a brief encounter at a graduation ceremony; there was something else about him Adam felt he should remember.

"How's your brother doing these days," Jones added.

"Brother? I don't have a brother Mr. Jones," Adam replied, a little surprised by the question.

"Really?" Jones responded with his own look of surprise. "I could have sworn Patrick told me about a brother."

"No sir. As far as I know I was an only child."

"As far as you know?" he quickly asked.

"I was adopted, Mr. Jones. My parents died in a boating accident when I was only three years old. My grandmother took me in until I was seven. After she died, Neil MacGregor adopted me. I've never asked, but I'm sure if I had a brother someone would have told me."

Something about the way the man was staring at him. Embracing each syllable as if hidden somewhere in the syntax of his words, Adam as about to reveal the meaning of life.

"Of course they would have," Jones said. "I'm sorry Adam, I must have you confused with another of Patrick's friends."

"It's all right Mr. Jones, but I'm afraid my lunch break is just about over. He may be my father, but today he's my boss as well. If you'll excuse me sir, it was a pleasure seeing you again," Adam said, as he stood.

As they shook hands, Jones leaned a little closer to Adam and said "Life's funny sometimes Adam, and sometimes it's just plain cruel. Take care of yourself."

Taken back not only by the statement, but also with the sincerity, in which it was spoken, Adam stood silent for a moment. Their eyes met and held tight to one another.

What was it about Peter Jones that seemed so familiar, yet distant. In that second or two of intense silence, Adam felt a kindred spirit with the stranger, an intimacy usually shared with long-time friends or family members. Letting go of the handshake, Adam numbly replied, "You too Mr. Jones."

Stepping out onto the cobblestone sidewalk, Adam took a deep breath of cold winter air, and began his walk back to South Station.

Throwing a dollar bill onto the counter, the man with the dark sunglasses, Celtics cap and jacket also left the deli, heading back toward South Station.

****

The moment Rick Goodwin pulled open the door to the office suite on the thirteenth floor, across the street from MacGregor and Son law firm, he knew there had been a development in the case. With the aid of high-tech surveillance equipment, two computer modules, several phones, three faxes, and a generous budget, he and his partner, Bob Thomas, were assigned the task of trailing Adam MacGregor.

He returned from his lunch at Lenny's Deli expecting to find Thomas reading some trashy magazine or wasting time on one of the hand-held computer games, but instead found him on the phone directly linked to the FBI's Deputy Director's office. The fax machine in the back was clicking rapidly, spewing forth a pile of documents.

He slid his dark sunglasses into his shirt pocket and removed his Celtics cap and Celtics jacket, tossing them carelessly over the back of a chair. Thomas waved him over to the desk and showed him a piece of paper on which he had been taking notes. Goodwin frowned at the information, thinking the man's handwriting was as scrambled as his thought process. As Goodwin tried deciphering the notes, Thomas handed him the phone.

"He wants to talk to you," he said, rising from his seat.

Goodwin waited while Thomas made himself comfortable behind one of the metal desks and began flipping through the latest issue of the National Enquirer. Some lady on the cover claimed to have given birth to an alien child with an uncanny resemblance to Elvis.

"Goodwin here sir," he said respectively, shaking his head in disgust at his partner's interest in such trash.

"Rick, it looks like our boy struck again. Columbian drug lord by the name of Santiago. Ever hear of him?" the Deputy drawled in his slow southern accent.

Deputy Director Richard Quinn was a native cracker, born and raised in Southern Georgia. He had been the deputy Director of the FBI for twelve years, and after the previous director was forced to resign under cloud of controversy, it was widely assumed Quinn would step into the position. However, a relative unknown named Eugene Polanik was named successor, thus overlooking one of the most honest, hard-working administrators in the Bureau.

"Eduard Santiago?" Goodwin answered, a little insulted the Deputy would even have to ask. "Of course I've heard of him sir. What have you got?" he added, while lighting a cigarette.

"Assassination. Columbian police are calling it an outside hit, but our boys in intelligence are painting a different picture. There were eight armed guards patrolling the outside perimeter, six more inside the house and all carrying modified SIG's, not to mention a security system better than the one protecting the President of the United States. Yet there were no signs of forced entry, no witnesses, and no suspects."

"What's coming over the fax?" Goodwin asked, while scribbling his own, more legible notes.

"Statements from the guards, Columbian police, and two still photos taken from a security camera on the second floor hallway. I think you'll find those most interesting. Take a look through and get back to me in about an hour. Remember to use the scrambler."

"You still think Director Polanik is getting wise to our operation?"

"The man's an idiot, Rick, but he's obviously connected. When we uncover Omega, I have no doubt a trail will somehow lead back to our beloved Director," he said, not trying to hide his bitterness.

Goodwin agreed and after hanging up the phone, made his way to the far corner of the room where the fax machines were located. Thomas was scanning a new article about a farmer in Idaho who claimed his pig could speak fluent French, calculate pie, and predict earthquakes in California. Goodwin would have been amused if Thomas weren't so engrossed by the story.

"You interested in any of this," Goodwin asked his partner, already knowing the answer.

"Not unless it's an order to kill somebody," Thomas said with a smirk, his eyes never leaving the paper.

Fighting back the urge to remove his service revolver and kill someone himself, Goodwin reached down for the documents instead.

At the fax machine sat eight documents in all. Goodwin glanced at the statements taken from the guards as well as the reports from the Columbian police, scanning them quickly. When he reached the final two sheets, still photos taken by a security camera on the second floor hallway of Santiago's home, he studied them closely, one in each hand.

Finishing the article detailing eyewitness accounts of Bigfoot at a Minnesota shopping mall, Thomas joined his partner at the desk.

"Hey, isn't that the guy we're suppose to be trailing," Thomas asked, while peering over Goodwin's shoulder.

"Yeah," Goodwin said softly. "Adam MacGregor."

"Mac, you have to believe me," the Senator pleaded. "As impossible as it sounds, I swear to you it's the truth."

Vigorously massaging his temples, his elbow firmly planted on the arms of the Victorian chair; Mac couldn't bring himself to look into the eyes of his longtime friend. The revelations the Senator had laid out before him were more likely to have been confessed by a conspiratorial junkie from an Oliver Stone movie than from a highly respected politician like Robert Allsworth.

"Bob," Mac began slowly, "You have to put yourself in my position. The accusations you're making, the story you're telling me, they're just...just unbelievable."

Allsworth rose from his chair and stiffly made his way to the complimentary wet bar in the back of the room. Refilling his glass for the second time, he quickly emptied it with one gulp.

"Bob slow down," Mac said. "It's not that I don't believe you, it's just I need time to understand. I'm an old-fashioned guy. I believe in government by the people, for the people. I believe in apple pie and Sunday softball games. I believe everyone is innocent until proven guilty. You can't expect me to suddenly change beliefs and accept this story of a vigilante Organization more powerful than our own government. An Organization run by highly placed and influential politicians and businessmen. And especially not some secret Organization with the scientific and technical breakthroughs you're talking about."

The Senator nodded; keeping his eyes fixed on the near-empty glass in his hand. "I know how you feel, Mac. I had the same reservations when they first approached me some twenty or so years ago," the Senator said, as he reclaimed his seat.

"Back then I was in pretty much the same political fight I find myself in now. Only this time I don't care if I win or lose, only that I come clean before it's too late."

This time it was Mac who made the short walk to the wet bar. Pouring a shot of whiskey, he turned to the Senator, who looked at him like a lost child reaching out for help.

"You say these people guaranteed you a lifetime seat in the U.S. Senate in return for your support."

"Not only a permanent seat Mac, but a chairmanship on a very influential committee. Twenty years ago, before all this talk about balanced budget amendments, the Finance Committee had unlimited discretion over whom received government grants and how much they received. The Organization used several phony pharmaceutical and medical corporations as a front for receiving millions of tax free dollars. Their research in genetic engineering was decades ahead of its time and getting more sophisticated every day. At first, my support for their work in return for what they were offering seemed a small price to pay. Every prospectus they sent me detailed in great length their desire to rid humanity of genetic diseases ranging from cancer to mental retardation.

"Hell I'd convinced myself that the cause was pure and in no way had I compromised my integrity. They deserved the money and any laurels that came with it," he said with a smirk.

"What happened then? How did this Organization become so corrupt?" Mac asked.

The Senator finished the last of his drink and handed Mac the glass indicating a refill.

"Greed, power, and a misdirected sense of justice. The usual vices which turn good men into something different. A few years after I became involved, they had a major breakthrough in their genetic research. Doctor Martin West, the senior geneticist had formulated a stand of DNA pure of any contaminants found in human cells. So pure and so perfect, that the possibilities were limitless. West wanted to go public immediately, but the Organization insisted it needed to test the sample, have proof of its pureness. West's own wife was used as the host mother."

"Martin West," Mac interrupted. "The Nobel Laureate for Genetic Science?" he asked skeptically.

"The same," Allsworth said before inhaling another sip of scotch.

"He and his wife were killed in a boating accident fifteen, twenty years ago. You're telling me he was part of this Organization?"

"He was the Organization Mac. Without West's breakthroughs in genetics, things never would have reached the level they're at today. And his death was no accident," the Senator added in a way which left no doubt about his accusation.

"The DNA. What happened to the sample?"

"The report I'm preparing for FBI's Deputy Director pretty much describes everything from the creatures they've created to as many influential members that I know about. But I need your help Mac. I don't know who Omega is, but what I do know will make Watergate look silly in comparison. I need you to represent my family and me when this hits the media and to protect me if I live long enough to testify. Mac, you're the only one I trust."

CHAPTER *Seven*

The moderate snowfall that began only an hour or so ago joined forces with a growing wind to add momentum to its citywide onslaught. Stretched out on the sofa with his feet crossed on the coffee table, Adam stared blankly out his office window thirteen floors above the snow-covered landscape. He returned from lunch shortly after one, only to find Mac still had not returned from his meeting with the Senator.

With nothing more to do but dwell on his current dilemma, he continued his decent into self-pity and depression.

What if all he was suffering from was a case of cold feet?

Perhaps he really did love Allison and his infatuation with Paige was nothing more than an escape clause.

Suppose he did break off his engagement and discovered too late he really did love Allison?

What if, by being afraid to make a commitment, he was jeopardizing his one real chance at happiness?

What if the moon was made out of green cheese and God was really some alien misfit named Fred?

No matter how many scenarios he devised to convince himself he was making a mistake, he knew he wasn't. Regardless of the pain and humiliation, he knew he would have to end his relationship with Allison Allsworth before Saturday night. If nothing else were to develop between him and Paige, then so be it. He would at least be out of an unpleasant relationship and no doubt still have Paige as a good friend.

He removed his feet from the coffee table and stood from the couch intending to first call Allison, then Paige. Or maybe Paige first and then Allison. Or maybe a stiff drink first, then think about it longer.

Before he could decide or even take his first step, he was sent cascading backward by a tidal wave of unexplained fear. The air suddenly compressed to the point of liquefaction and it became almost impossible for his lungs to fully recover from the initial shock. An undertow of terror began pulling him further into the darkness of a bottomless sea. He thought he would suffocate before the attack ended. He wanted to fall to the carpet, possibly crawl to the door, cry for help, or scream. Anything but the overwhelming and debilitating sense of helplessness that left him paralyzed only moments ago.

Involuntarily, he let out a pitiful whelp, barely discernible even to himself.

Then, as quickly and as unexpectantly as the wave crashed into him, it left him. Feeding his lungs as quickly as possible, almost hyperventilating, Adam braced himself for another attack.

He sat rigid on the sofa, staring past the whiteness outside, concentrating instead on the blackness that had just stained his insides. The swirling flakes, blowing left then right, had a hypnotic effect and soon his mind, as well as his vision, became clouded.

He was no longer sitting on the sofa in a plush law firm in downtown Boston. Instead, he was drifting aimlessly back in time, toward events he had no memory of experiencing.

A young boy on Christmas morning, though there was no reference to the holiday, he somehow knew it was Christmas. The same way he knew he was the little boy.

A light snowfall, similar to the one that began hours ago. An elderly woman he thought was his grandmother, but for some reason had remembered differently.

A farmhouse...somewhere, he couldn't remember where.

As his subconscious mind forced him down memory lane, he couldn't be sure if the events were real or imagined. Somehow though, he sensed he should remember, should have some recollection of the scenes being played out before him.

The little boy surveyed the snow-covered grounds with an air of expectancy. Feelings of excitement and anticipation coursed freely though Adam's body.

Suddenly, he was jolted from the picturesque, snow-draped farmhouse with frightening clarity.

He was outdoors now, in front of a barn, staring at the flame-engulfed farmhouse.

New, stronger feelings began to overwhelm him.

Fear. Helplessness. Panic.

Framed in the small attic window, four floors above, was his grandmother, or at least the person he thought was his grandmother. She was frantically pounding her clenched fists against the clapboards, screaming for help.

Adam wanted to break free from the vision, snap out of a bad daydream, but an instant before he could will himself to do so; he saw something even more horrifying than his grandmother burning in the flames.

He saw himself.

Though that was impossible, since he was still watching the surreal nightmare from the ground below.

Then who or what was smiling down upon him from the attic window?

"Adam," the voice said, betraying a tone mixed with fear and worry. "Adam, are you all right?"

He recognized the voice as that of his secretary, Donna Cabral. At forty-nine, Donna suffered every ailment known to medicine and then some. In addition to being a hypochondriac, the office gossip, and general pain in the ass, she was additionally blessed with the gift of always knowing everything, whether it was right or not.

As his eyes began to focus on the surroundings of his office, he noticed his bare white knuckles clutching viciously to the cushions of the sofa. He felt a thin bead of perspiration tingle across his forehead and the discomfort in his jaw from clenching his teeth, as though he had been strapped into a runaway roller coaster.

"My God, Adam, what's wrong? What's happening?" Donna asked again.

Adam wished he could tell her, but he wasn't sure what happened or was still happening. Although he was out of his trance, scenes of a past life, with people and places he'd never seen or visited still ran untamed though his mind.

"I...I must have ate some bad food or something at lunch," he lied, hoping it sounded convincing. He didn't need Donna telling anyone who would listen about the firm's new partner losing his grip.

"Oh, you know, I bet you're right," Donna answered, eager to continue. "My sister, Louise, the one down in Alabama, you know, the one married to the Elvis impersonator. Well, not really, he's a truck driver, but every now and then he does a benefit for the local Knights of Columbus. I saw him do this act once a couple of years ago when I visited them. Not bad really. Anyway, my sister, Louise, she got food poisoning last year. Oh Adam, I'm telling you as sure as I'm standing here, if she could have chosen death she would have. Her face was...."

"Donna," Adam interrupted sharply, as soon as she paused for air. 'I appreciate your concern, but I'm really not feeling very well. Would you mind bringing me a couple of aspirins?"

"Of course not," she said pleasantly, apparently not offended at having her story cut short. "I'll be right back."

As he watched her hurried exit, Adam cautiously lifted himself from the sofa and groped the corner of his desk for support.

Then the wave broke, hitting him again.

A hospital room.

The same little boy or was it the one in the window, he couldn't be sure, was strapped to a metal gurney.

Doctors, lab technicians, three men in suits.

A needle.

A scream.

He sat behind his desk, unsure of how he got there, but grateful to be back in the present.

The thin bead of perspiration that formed across his forehead had begun a lazy trickle down past his right temple. He wanted to wipe his brow, but was afraid to let go of the desk he was so feverishly gripping.

"What the hell's happening to me?" he asked with difficulty.

✳✳✳✳✳✳✳✳✳✳✳✳✳✳✳✳✳✳✳✳✳✳✳✳✳✳✳✳✳✳✳✳✳✳✳✳

Allison spent the afternoon with several caterers; all offering unique and exquisite selections, all responding like whipped dogs at the snap of her fingers. The power and control she wielded over commoners such as these was as exhilarating as sex and even more satisfying.

"We would, of course, be able to alter our entire menu to suit your personal tastes, Ms. Allsworth," one of them offered.

"Our chef, Pierre LeCroart, has served in some of the finest French quarters," another began. "At one time he was even the personal chef for President Francois Mitterand of France," he added in hopes of impressing her.

"Naturally, anything Madam requests out of the standard package would be honored at no additional charge," still a third man with a European accent promised.

Allison thanked them for their time, promised to get back to them shortly, and casually dismissed them from her presence.

So much work, so many decisions, she thought.

Once married, the word **work** would be forbidden from her household. Adam would take care of any problems with the domestics, while she spent her days and his money at the most fashionable boutiques, having lunch with friends at the choicest restaurants, and relaxing in the afternoon at the most exclusive clubs.

It wasn't as though she didn't deserve the lifestyle she had so carefully planned. Gazing admirably at her reflection in the mirror, Allison was, as usual, amazed by her own beauty.

Her jet-black hair was curled perfectly just below her perfectly formed shoulders. Her dark eyes were large, seductive and spaced perfectly on either side of a perfect nose. Her full, red lips gave way to a perfect smile, and there was no denying her long slender figure was perfectly proportioned.

Indeed, Adam MacGregor was a very lucky man.

Soon, with her guidance, he would be a very successful one also.

Not only had Allison mapped out her future, but she had been considerate enough to map out her fiancé's as well. It was just one of the many things Adam would come to appreciate.

Within seven or eight years of working fourteen to sixteen hours a day, six or seven days a week, Adam should have built himself a very profitable practice with a very respectable clientele. Then, with her father's clout and direction, Adam would enter the political arena. Of course, it wouldn't be anything too glamorous at first. Perhaps a congressman or a state senator.

After a few years of devoted public service though, he could elevate himself into the national spotlight. A United States Senator like her father or maybe Governor of the great State of Massachusetts.

A few more years of ardent service for the good of the public, encompassing long hours dedicated to the final goal: President of the United States.

All the while, she would be sharing the spotlight. The beautiful wife, the strength behind the man. The most envied woman in the country. The next Jacqueline Kennedy.

First Lady Allison MacGregor.

It was all so wonderful. So well thought out. As perfect in theory as she was in physical beauty.

The weather outside had gone from gray to white as the snow made its way from the sky above. The room itself was cozy though, as the wall-length fireplace crackled with heat. Still reveling in the euphoric effects of her future, she was suddenly overcome by a frequent need. She called for Charles to bring her the phone though it laid on a marble stand less than ten feet from where she rested.

Stretching the length of the sofa, she waited for the servant to close the study doors before she dialed a number she knew by heart. On the third ring, a man answered.

"Tennis club, Paul speaking."

"Afternoon lover," she whispered seductively. "I've been so lonely this morning I could die. How would you like to make me feel special?" she asked, already knowing his response.

Without missing a beat, the man replied quickly, "The guest house at three."

"Perfect," she purred

Chapter *Eight*

"How's that possible though sir?" Goodwin asked. "I was sitting across from him at the deli during the time Santiago was assassinated."

After thoroughly reviewing the faxed report from the Deputy Director, Goodwin compiled a list of questions and comments before using the scrambler to call back his superior.

"How's any of it possible Rick? Dr. West's private diary that our mystery man sent us states some pretty amazing things. Combine that with Senator Allsworth's phone call this morning and you have something right from the pages of a Stephen King novel."

"Any leads on who this mystery informer is, sir?"

"Nothing concrete, but he's been pretty accurate so far with his information. His main concern is for the safety of Adam MacGregor. So for the time being, we'll play by his rules. How are things on your end?"

"Thomas bugged MacGregor's house and car earlier this morning, and the office will be bugged later tonight. This weather's playing havoc with our directional microphone, but we were able to pick up a conversation he had with a Doctor Jellison's office in Brookline. Apparently, he's a general practitioner."

"A doctor huh. Any idea why?"

"No. He was pretty vague on the phone. Said he wanted to come in for his yearly physical. But shortly after making the appointment, he began acting rather strange. Claims it's food poisoning or something."

"Hmm," the Deputy drawled. "Well I expect to hear from our informer at some point today. Maybe he can shed some light on the

MacGregor kid's role in this Organization. Until we know for sure though what his connection is, I want you to follow him as closely as possible. Treat him as you would any dangerous suspect."

"Do you want him apprehended at any point? Maybe question him in a round-about way?"

"No, we'd better not. Let's go with surveillance only. If the kid is somehow involved, we don't want to tip our hand. And Rick, try to keep Thomas in line. We don't need some trigger-happy agent blowing our cover."

For a moment, Goodwin thought of his own urge to shoot his partner earlier and smiled.

"I'll do my best sir."

✱✱✱✱✱✱✱✱✱✱✱✱✱✱✱✱✱✱✱✱✱✱✱✱✱✱✱✱✱✱✱✱✱✱✱✱

By two o'clock, the lunch crowd had begun to disappear. Paige began circulating the small cafeteria, greeting the homeless men and women who lingered behind.

The clattering of dishes and the banging of pots and pans from the kitchen echoed loudly through the room. Her foul mood, which had wrapped itself tightly around her bones that morning, had only gotten darker after Adam's phone call. Her one saving grace to the day, her dinner date with him that evening, had been postponed.

Adam blamed it on the weather and an unusual amount of research for his first case. He promised that regardless of the weather or who his next client was, they would have their celebration dinner tomorrow evening.

Tomorrow. The next day. The day after that.

What did it matter?

She was only fooling herself into thinking there could ever be more between them than the friendship they shared. Adam was in love with Allison, and by that weekend, he would officially be engaged to her and shortly thereafter become her husband. In a few short years, there would be a little Adam or a little Allison running around the MacGregor household calling her Auntie Paige instead of mommy.

Trying to keep from being swallowed by envy, she casually approached a man sitting by himself, nursing the remains of his soup and sandwich. He looked lonely and sad, feelings she could relate to on a personal level. She straightened up, forcing herself to put her problems into context with those around her.

She might be the victim of an unrequited love, but at least she had more going for her than the poor souls who made their way into the shelter. She at least had a place to call home, friends who loved her, and a career she felt made a difference.

She pulled out a chair next to the man and sat beside him. "Good afternoon," she said with a forced smile. "I'm Paige Allsworth, a counselor at the shelter."

The man carefully rested his spoon in the soup bowl and held out his hand.

"A pleasure to make your acquaintance Ms. Allsworth. I'm Peter Jones, a guest of your shelter," he said, holding out his right hand.

"The pleasure is all mine Mr. Jones. Will you be staying the night with us?" she asked cordially.

"Ah, my dear," he began as though he was performing on stage. "For so many years I have longed to hear a woman as beautiful as yourself ask me if I wanted to spend the night. Alas, I'm afraid I'll have to take a raincheck. Other obligations, you understand."

Paige learned a great deal about the psychological make-up of the homeless men and women who visited the shelter. The one common denominator in most of them was pride. They didn't like the idea of taking handouts or accepting charity. They had a need to remain as independent as possible, coming in only when the elements of nature or the emptiness of their bellies became too great. She was sure the only other obligation Peter Jones had for the evening was securing his place next to a warm fire or inside an abandoned building.

"Mr. Jones, unless those other obligations involve a warm shelter and a hot meal, I'd strongly urge you to reschedule. The storm's only going to get worse as nightfall approaches."

"It's difficult for a man to resist the generous offer of such a kind woman. Even a man with only one arm," he said, patting his left side with his right hand. "I assure you I'll give it some thought."

For a moment they only looked at one another and finally he said, "Tell me Ms. Allsworth, if it's not too personal, why is a woman as lovely as yourself so downtrodden today? A man, perhaps," he said with a sly wink. "Love can be a double-edged sword at times."

Caught completely off guard by the question, Paige felt the burning redness of her cheeks, as she stammered for a reply.

"I'm sorry, my dear. I see I've embarrassed you with my forwardness. I do apologize," he said before she could answer.

"No, don't be silly. I'm not embarrassed," she said with her face still flushed.

"Then humor an old man. Tell me who this person is that's so blind as not to see what a charming lady you are?"

Paige smiled, the compliment only heightening her embarrassment.

"Mr. Jones I'm flattered that you take an interest in my personal life, but I'm not sure this is the time or place to be discussing my problems. As a matter of fact, this is the time and place to be discussing your problems. So tell me, honestly, do you have a place to stay this evening? It's going to drop well below freezing tonight."

"I'll make a deal with you Ms. Allsworth. I'll agree to come in from the cold, so to speak, in return for your company at dinner this evening. I know a quaint little shelter that serves a marvelous minestrone soup and tuna fish sandwich," he said with a boyish grin.

A grin that appeared deceptively familiar though where she had seen it or on who, she couldn't quite be sure.

"As it turns out Mr. Jones, my plans for this evening were abruptly changed. I'd be honored to be your companion for dinner," she said with her own juvenile grin.

Peter Jones stood, placed his gray fedora on his head, and smiled.

"I shall return later this evening then my dear. Good day," he said with a flamboyant bow.

Exiting the shelter, Jones walked a block and a half south and took a left into a vacant lot.

Within a minute, the black stretch limousine pulled up beside him, and the driver quickly opened the rear door.

"Thank you William," Peter Jones said, as he crawled inside.

"Your welcome sir," the driver answered.

CHAPTER *Nine*

"Flashbacks," Omega hollered into the phone. "What the hell do you mean flashbacks."

Though Alec had been successful in his assassination of Eduard Santiago, it had been necessary for Wenzler to keep him sedated since his return.

"It's complicated Omega, but in layman's terms, the memory block we installed in him as a child is beginning to crack. He's beginning to remember who he was. That's why he's having these uncontrollable fits of rage. It's his subconscious way of dealing with the breakthrough. It's going to be necessary to retrain and reprogram him," Doctor Wenzler explained.

Since the death of Martin West and his wife almost two decades earlier, Wenzler and Omega had argued, fought, and bitterly disagreed over every detail of Alec's upbringing. Using manipulative brain techniques thought inhumane and unsafe by the medical community, Wenzler successfully altered and erased Alec's subconscious memory. In the massless void that remained, he was able to create an entirely different memory with values and beliefs solely in the interest of the Organization. In essence, he wiped clean one existence and replaced it with another, more cooperative, robotic existence.

Though the unprecedented procedure was successful, it took close to a year to bring Alec's powers of teleportation and perfected immune system back to the level he previously attained. That was the concern Omega had with reprogramming him now.

"We can't do it yet," Omega said. "We need to send Alec on one more mission. We can't afford the luxury of being without his talents for up to twelve months."

Wenzler let the silence hang between them like a heavy fog. Once again, he could feel his authority being undermined.

"With all due respect Omega, as Director of Research and Development, I believe it's my decision whether Alec is capable of performing another mission," Wenzler said boldly. "And based on what I've seen today and know to be true, I will recommend to the Board that we begin reprogramming immediately."

"Very well put Doctor. Normally I'd be forced to accept your recommendation. However, I'm afraid the Organization has a very serious threat to its anonymity. And unless that threat is put to rest permanently, there won't be any Board to present your precious recommendation to. And based on what I've seen today and know to be true, Doctor," he added, letting the words dangle for a moment, "unless you agree with me, there won't be a Research and Development Department for you to play God with either."

The threat of a mole or informer always intimidated the Board just enough so they sided with elimination over research.

Feeling it was time to play his trump card, Wenzler very calmly said, "Very well Omega. But might I remind you, if Alec is suffering a memory collapse, you know who else is probably feeling them as well."

The words slammed into Omega so hard it left him momentarily breathless. Long ago the connection between Alec and Adam ceased to exist. He loved them both very much, but for very different reasons.

For Alec, he was Omega, head of a powerful Organization but also a caring, loving force in his life. With others in the Organization, he raised Alec, taught him the principles and guidelines he needed to learn, cared for him when the experiments went badly, held him when the thresholds of pain were greater than his advanced immune system could tolerate. Always though, he did it with the Organization's best interest at heart.

The day Adam West became Adam MacGregor was the last time Omega thought of him as an experiment and began loving him as a son.

To Adam, he was Neil MacGregor. Mac. Dad.

With Adam, everything he did was from a primitive need to nurture. Compassion and love Mac never thought he would feel again after his wife's brutal death, he gave freely to his adoptive son. To be reminded after all these years of the unbreakable bond of brotherhood was a devastating blow. To realize the weakness in Alec was more than likely a weakness in Adam left him numb and speechless.

His prolonged silence was all the satisfaction Wenzler needed, for now.

Chapter *Ten*

Still confused and frightened by the strange occurrence in his office earlier, Adam decided not to risk driving his own car and instead hailed a cab to meet his new client at the Charles Street Jail. His appointment with Doctor Jellison was at the Massachusetts General Hospital at four o'clock, only a half a block from the prison. A brisk afternoon walk might help him figure out what the hell happened to him earlier.

The Charles Street Jail was a medium-security facility, which served also as a holding block for alleged criminals awaiting trial or sentencing. One of the oldest jails in Massachusetts, it looked every bit its one hundred and twenty years. An obligatory plaque hung on rusted hinges outside the main gate. On it were listed the date of completion, the name of the governor back then, the names of long-forgotten politicians and businessmen who were instrumental in its completion and the names of the architect and contractor. It was a state-of-the-art facility when it was built, but the immediate area surrounding the jail progressed along with the times and the old red bricked building was now more of an eye-sore than an eye-pleaser. The ten-foot brick wall that circled the yard was topped with thick strands of barbed wire and a menacing roll of shiny razor wire. Four identical towers with glass enclosed cubes on top, stood high above the facility at each of its corners.

The administration building was located just outside the main gate, and Adam was able to walk in without any obstruction. It was a single-story brick structure that housed fourteen different administrative offices. The one Adam sought was at the end of a long gray corridor.

The half wood, half glass door was slightly ajar, and Adam eased it opened, as he knocked lightly on the glass half.

"I don't give a shit how crowded Walpole is. I have transfer orders here for thirty-seven inmates and transfer them is what I intend to do. The Sheriff's office is here now, and these boys will be your responsibility in about fifty minutes," an overweight, over-worked civil employee was angrily shouting into the phone.

Walpole State Prison was the state's maximum-security facility. At last estimate it was said to be housing more than forty percent its capacity.

The man hung up the phone and stared at Adam.

"Well," he asked impatiently.

"Excuse me," Adam began. "I was told to check with you about getting a visitor's pass to see my client."

"You an attorney," he asked while pulling open one of his desk drawers.

"Yes sir," Adam answered, placing his business card and the court order on the man's desk.

"I don't need that," he said pushing them away. "Who you here to see?" he asked.

"Green, David."

The man filled out the paperwork in longhand and handed Adam a pass. "Give this to the guard at the main gate."

The man picked up the phone and quickly dialed seven digits. Looking up at Adam, he made a motion with his hand to wave him away.

At the main gate, a guard with arms the size of Adam's thighs greeted him with a grunt. He glanced quickly at the pass and directed Adam to the second of two red-bricked buildings.

"You can wait in there. They'll bring your boy around shortly," he said without making eye contact.

Once inside, he handed his briefcase to another guard, who placed it on a roller, and watched as it slid under the x-ray machine. Walking through the metal detector, he retrieved his case on the other side.

"Pick a seat," the guard said.

There were no other lawyers or visitors in the small conference room, and Adam sat at the chair furthest from the door.

The room was chilly. The heating system growled angrily and produced much less warmth than it should. Nevertheless, Adam removed his coat and draped it over the chair next to him.

In front of him was a three-foot brick wall topped by a Formica counter and from there a triple pane bulletproof glass ran to the ceiling. Phones were placed evenly on either side.

A door bolt clicked, and the sound of heavy iron doors echoed in the empty room.

David Green and a towering black guard stepped forward. Green looked about forty, but his arrest sheet said he was fifty-three. A shock of black hair as dark as his eyes and only slightly lighter than his skin gave him an eerie possessed aura.

Adam picked up the phone and waited for his client to do the same. Green pulled out a chair and stared at his attorney. He reached into his pocket, removed a genetic cigarette, and lit it slowly. The flame flickered and danced in his black eyes like a demonic ritual.

After taking a deep drag, he exhaled and picked up his end of the receiver.

"Mr. Green, if you want me to help you, I'm going to need your cooperation. There are several questions I need answered and even more petitions I need to prepare."

Another deep drag and more silence.

Adam tried to appear as cool and nonchalant as his client, but knew the act fell short of convincing. He'd hoped not to appear as rattled or as nervous as he felt. Thirty seconds passed without a word, though it felt more like thirty minutes.

Finally, Green leaned into the window with a menacing stare and asked "What's the matter boy, you got a porcupine up your ass or something?"

"Beg your pardon?" Adam asked a little embarrassed by the question.

"Stop fidgeting about. You're starting to make *me* nervous. How old are you anyway, boy?"

"Does my age matter, Mr. Green? I'm an attorney, and I'm here to offer you my assistance. If you'd like, you may petition the court for a different public defender. I'd be happy to submit the paperwork for you."

Green suddenly burst into laughter. "You white boys are all alike," he said between laughs. "You see a nigger and you get all flustered. I asked you a simple question, and now you're all bent out of shape. How old are you, twenty-five, twenty-six?"

"I'm twenty-eight, Mr. Green. Now I want to ask you about the night you were arrested."

"How long you been a lawyer?" Green asked without acknowledging Adam's last question.

"The truth Mr. Green, is that today is my first day as a practicing attorney in the State of Massachusetts. I attended Yale Law School and graduated first in my class. I've worked as a paralegal for the last three years at MacGregor and Associates, and you are my first client. If you're comfortable with that, I'd like to start the interview."

Green erupted into a hardy laugh and stamped out his cigarette.

"I like you boy. You got balls, I can tell. And I'll take a set of iron balls over experience any day. Okay, what's the first thing we got to do to get my sorry black ass out of here?"

Though Adam could feel every pore in his body beginning to ooze sweat and his stomach rested somewhere around his throat he was beginning to feel like an attorney. He had won over his first client.

"The first thing, Mr. Green is…."

"David. Call me David."

"Very well David. The first thing is…."

"And what should I call you?"

"Adam. You can call me Adam."

"All right Adam, enough of this small talk. Time is money. How you gonna get me out of here?"

Adam couldn't help but smile. David Green was very colorful indeed.

"The first thing I need to know is exactly what happened the night they arrested you, and Mr....er...David, anything but the truth is only going to complicate our case," Adam said.

"Hey, I might be a lot of things to a lot of people, boy, but I ain't no liar," Green said proudly. Lighting another cigarette he continued, "Them damn cops been trying to bust me for months. Every night when I leave my place of business, there's at least one cruiser outside watching me. Saturday night was no different. About half-mile from my club, I get pulled over by a couple of white bread, panty-ass cops. They say I took a left turn without using my blinker. You believe that shit, no blinker."

"Did you use your blinker?" Adam interrupted, only because he felt he should ask something.

"Hell boy, how do I know? Anyways, one of them cops, he tells me to get out of the car and spread my legs. Says I know the routine. The next thing I'm in handcuffs and being thrown into the back of the cruiser. The second cop, he just takes my car keys and opens my trunk. And presto, I'm back in jail awaiting trial for illegal gun possession."

Adam finished taking notes and looked up at his client.

"The police didn't ask your permission to look in the trunk?"

"Christ Sakes boy, do you think I would have given them permission knowing what was in there? They didn't ask me shit," Green said defiantly.

"Did they have any reason to search the car? Any drug paraphernalia or weapons in plain sight? Anything at all that would give them probable cause to suspect a crime had been committed?" Adam asked intently.

"I'm a nigger with a rap sheet who owns a sleazy strip bar. That's all the probable cause they need."

"No David, that's not all they need. I'm meeting with the Assistant D.A. tomorrow morning and I'll talk with the arresting officers sometime before your arraignment. If what you tell me is true, I think we can get you out of here sooner than you think."

✶✶✶✶✶✶✶✶✶✶✶✶✶✶✶✶✶✶✶✶✶✶✶✶✶✶✶✶✶✶✶✶✶✶✶✶

Deputy Director Quinn stared down at the avalanche of paperwork that seemed to grow spontaneously from his desk.

In the twelve years he served in the administrative capacity, he had seen the FBI's budget soar past the one billion dollar per year plateau.

The fifty-eight field offices throughout the United States and Puerto Rico employed more than twenty-one thousand people, nine thousand of whom served as special agents.

He was reading through the latest interoffice memo sent by the Director concerning more of the usual bureaucratic nonsense when his private line began to ring.

"Quinn," he said, while reaching for his notepad and pen. Nobody called his private line without have something important to report.

"Did it happen?" the voice asked.

Though the man was speaking through a scrambler, not only to disguise his voice, but also to prevent his call from being traced, Quinn knew immediately to whom he was speaking.

"Just as you said it would. Santiago was assassinated earlier today."

Quinn quickly turned to the section of the notepad already entitled MYSTERY MAN and flipped to an empty page. In the two weeks he had known about the existence of the mystery informer, he had already been able to solicit some information concerning his identity. He estimated the man to be in his late fifties to early sixties, very intelligent, and he was a man of substantial means. Also, in one of their initial conversations, the man let it be known he was without the benefit of his left arm.

"Two others are scheduled for elimination sometime today. Jesse Diego and John Caleb are both habitual criminals and probably deserve what the Organization has in store for them," the man said calmly.

"You sound like you condone their activities."

"If I condoned their activities Mr. Quinn, I would never have sent you Martin West's private diary or leaked any of the information you've received so far. There's no room in society for an Organization that serves as judge and jury. I may not shed any tears for those they eliminate, but it doesn't mean I approve of their methods."

"Then why not simply tell us who these people are and where we can locate them. I could have two hundred agents ready in thirty minutes."

"The Organization doesn't have just one base of operations. As a matter of fact, they probably have just as many field offices as the FBI. But more importantly, Mr. Deputy Director, the Organization has on its payroll anywhere from a hundred to a hundred and fifty of the Bureau's agents, including the Director himself. You couldn't put together lunch without the Organization knowing about it first."

__A hundred to a hundred and fifty agents,__ Quinn thought.

"How do you know so much about them? Are you Omega?"

The man gave a quick chuckle before saying, "No, I'm not Omega. Nor am I part of them," he said disdainfully. "But I do have contacts who are still loyal to me and agree that the Organization has gone too far."

"Still loyal to you?" Quinn asked. "Does that mean you were once a part of them."

During the brief silence, Quinn was able to detect the muffled background noises of a horn, barely audible music, and the repetitive clicking of the scrambler. He jotted down the word car phone on his notepad, and since his informer had only one arm, Quinn assumed there was a driver with him. Next to the word car he wrote **limousine**.

"In many ways you could say I'm an unwitting part of the Organization and always will be."

"What about Adam MacGregor? You haven't told me why you want him tailed. Is he a part of the Organization?"

"No!" the man said forcefully. "You're not tailing him for information but for protection. I made that perfectly clear as one of the conditions for my assistance. He knows nothing about Omega or his merry band of vigilantes. It must remain that way or all bets are off," the man said in a threatening tone.

"It would help if we knew who we were protecting him from. Has he done something to the Organization to put his life in jeopardy?"

"His being alive poses more of a threat to the Organization than they realize. Very soon they'll recognize that threat and try to eliminate it one way or another."

"The man who assassinated Santiago, he was Adam's brother, wasn't he?" Quinn asked, pressing the issue.

Again silence and for a moment Quinn felt he pushed his informant too far, too fast.

"A rather speculative assumption, Mr. Quinn," the man finally said. "May I ask what brought you to such a conclusion?"

"Two months ago, Interpol sent us a description and artist's sketch of a man they say was responsible for the assassination of a Libyan terrorist named Abul Nurod. Both the sketch and the description fit Adam to a tee."

"As I'm sure you are well aware Mr. Quinn, artists' renditions based on the observations of third parties are rather subjective. I'm sure he could have drawn it a thousand other ways to match a thousand other people," he replied in a condescending tone.

"You have a point, sir. However, in Santiago's case, his assassin was caught on a security camera inside the home. There's little doubt that the Interpol description and sketch match the photos taken this morning. And there's even less doubt that the man in the photo is a dead ringer for Adam MacGregor."

Quinn paused long enough for his statement to have its full effect before continuing; "Adam is the other one discussed in West's diary, isn't he? The highly intelligent one," he said, quoting directly from the diary. "Yet lacking any of the astonishing breakthroughs in human development displayed by his sibling," he added, finishing the passage.

"I'll deliver you Omega and the Organization, Mr. Deputy Director. For your part, make sure nothing happens to Adam. I'll be in touch," the man said curtly before hanging up.

****

Chapter *Eleven*

Their lovemaking was in rhythm with Prince singing his hit song, "Little Red Corvette". Almost violently, they slammed into one another with uncontrolled passion and lust. As the song alluded to the woman's promiscuity, the man stiffened, clutched his lover in a tight grasp and let out a painful but satisfying groan.

"No, not yet, sweetheart. Not yet," she begged.

The man was helpless to her pleas though, finishing his orgasm before rolling off her onto his side of the bed.

"Oh Paul. I thought you were suppose to be the club stud," Allison said with a mixture of disappointment and sarcasm.

"Baby that's the third time this afternoon. Can I help it if you're insatiable? Give me twenty minutes and I'll be ready to bring you to new heights," he said in defense of his performance.

"I've heard that before. Besides it's almost four o'clock. You should be leaving, and I should be calling Adam."

In frustration, Paul flung the sheets from his naked body. "I can't believe you're gonna marry that guy. What's he got that I don't?" he asked in a hurt, childish voice.

"Besides a future, a promising career, a wealthy father, and unlimited potential, you're about equal," she said spitefully. "I can't tell you what a difficult decision it was for me Paul. A young successful lawyer with enough money and family ties to insure my lifestyle goes unchanged or an aging tennis pro with more bills than brains," she added for effect.

"You bitch! Maybe the boy wonder would be interested in knowing who his young bride-to-be has been fucking on a regular basis?" he threatened in a vain attempt to intimidate her. Allison simply rolled her eyes and got out of bed.

"Darling, please don't bore me with such trivial nonsense. We both know nobody would believe such a ridiculous claim. The daughter of a U.S. Senator, engaged to the son of an equally powerful man, sleeping around with none other than the club tennis pro. Sweetheart, you've been watching too many soap operas. Please, let's act like adults, shall we?" she said while admiring her naked body in front of the mirror. "Besides, just because I'm getting married, doesn't mean I'm not going to be needing your services any longer," she added, while giving him a flirtive smile.

Coming up from behind, he spun her around roughly and lifted her from the floor. Taking three steps back to the bed, he dropped her onto the mattress and straddled her waist. Pinning her arms over her shoulders with his, he slid his body between her already spread thighs.

"You drive me crazy, bitch. You know that?"

She smiled briefly, flicking her tongue into his mouth.

"Has it been twenty minutes already?" she said playfully, before he pushed himself up into her.

∗∗∗∗∗∗∗∗∗∗∗∗∗∗∗∗∗∗∗∗∗∗∗∗∗∗∗∗∗∗∗∗∗∗∗∗

Doctor Matthew Jellison's examination room at the Massachusetts General Hospital was one of three identical cubicles separated only by nylon drapes. Off-white walls, stainless steel fixtures, a scrub sink, a gray medicine cabinet, an eye chart, and several modern pieces of equipment filled out the small area. The heavy odor of disinfectant permeated the air.

What the examination rooms lacked in décor though, the doctors made up for in brilliance. Throughout the United States and most of the world, the reputation of the hospital and its staff was renown.

Adam sat nervously on the edge of the padded examination table. The roll of white sheeting paper crunched and crumpled with his every breath.

He was naked, save for the flimsy backless johnny that tied loosely around his chilled body. His palms were wet and his stomach felt as though a hundred caterpillars had simultaneously blossomed into full-fledged butterflies. It wasn't a fear of doctors that made him nervous; it was a fear of what they could diagnose.

A brain tumor.

Aneurysm.

A chemical imbalance responsible for early senility.

Adam's imagination ran uninhibited with possible self-diagnosed reasons for his behavior.

Determined not to sound like a raving lunatic, Adam described his symptoms in the same even, matter-of-fact tone he would use if addressing a jury. When possible, he used clinical terms rather than emotional ones, and he made a conscious effort not to appear worried his problems were anything but typical.

For the doctor's part, he listened carefully, making a note or two when he felt it necessary.

At sixty-three, he was one of the most sought-after internist in the country. Completely bald, with the exception of some very determined hair on the sides of his head, he had a face that naturally relaxed a patient. Just over six feel tall; his body was rugged and strong, his hands were enormous but gentle, and his smile was ever present.

For the past hour, Adam had undergone several testing procedures ranging from cat scans to x-rays to blood samples. Thankfully, all had come back negative.

"Deep breathe and hold it," Jellison said, as he placed the cold steel of the stethoscope to Adam's back. After repeating the procedure on his chest and apparently satisfied at what he heard, he told Adam to dress and meet him in his office.

Ten minutes later, Adam sat nervously in the high-back leather chair in front of Doctor Jellison.

"Just before the black-outs Adam, are there any strange smells, dizziness, blindness, anything out of the ordinary that you remember?" Jellison asked, now sitting behind a large oak desk.

Adam thought for a moment and said, "I really don't remember. On both occasions I only knew about the blackouts after they occurred. So I really can't say what I felt a minute or two before."

Jellison nodded, and Adam strained to see what he wrote in the medical chart.

"Any unusual stress or pressure in your life lately? Anything that you're uncomfortable about or worried over that may be occupying more of your thoughts than you'd like?"

Adam grimaced, as if jabbed with a sharp instrument. Not wanting to go too deep into his personal problems, he tried to remain as vague as possible.

"There have been a couple of issues lately that I've been worried about. Well, a little more than just worried, I guess."

Jellison made a couple of more notations then looked up at Adam. Placing the pen and chart to his left, he folded his hands in front of him, looking like a father about to explain the facts of life to his son.

"Adam, all your test results have come back negative. Which is good. It shows me there are no tumors, lesions, blood imbalances or clotting which may be putting pressure on surrounding brain tissue. To be honest Adam, you're as healthy as a horse. There are one or two test results, mostly blood work, that are still in the lab, but I'm sure we're going to draw a blank on those as well."

"I suppose I should be relieved, but I still don't have an explanation for what's been happening to me," Adam said, sounding slightly disappointed.

"I think I know what the cause may be Adam," Jellison said, removing a business card from his Rolodex. "Doctor Leppo is a friend of mine and very good in his field," he added, reaching across the desk to hand Adam the card.

"Doctor Ronald Leppo, Psychiatrist," Adam said reading from the card. "You think I'm crazy?" he asked, only half joking.

"Crazy, no. Stressed, yes. There's no physical explanation for your behavior Adam, at least none I can find. Dr. Leppo specializes in stress-related psychology. Seeing a psychiatrist doesn't infer you're crazy or on the verge of a breakdown. It simply means you need help expressing and dealing with subconscious conflicts. Conflicts, which in your case, could eventually lead to a physical problem. Now I can't force you to call him, but if you want my professional opinion, I'd suggest an appointment at your earliest convenience."

Adam stared down at the card, feeling slightly embarrassed about the turn of events. Nodding, he said, "I'll give it some thought Doctor. Thank you."

****

Chapter *Twelve*

At 7:15 PM, Mac turned into the freshly plowed parking lot of the Cambridge medical building. Three other vehicles, a vintage white BMW and two late model black Mercedes, were parked in the first three spots. Mac recognized the cars as belonging to other Board members of the Organization.

The Board members, some in person, some by way of satellite link-up, gathered on Judgment night to pass sentencing on the new list of felons which appeared on the computer printout. Tonight they would decide which names would be met by field teams and which would require Alec's assistance. Based on his earlier conversation with Dr. Wenzler, Mac already knew Alec would have only one assignment this month before undergoing extensive reprogramming: Senator Robert Allsworth.

For the first time in twenty-five years, Mac had deep regrets and sorrow in connection with a name on the Judgment list. He considered the Senator one of his closest friends. A man whose loyalty was instrumental to the financing of the Organization back when money was a concern, a man who would be related by marriage in a few short months, and a man that, until a few hours ago, Mac respected.

Life was nothing if not unpredictable.

Twenty-five years ago, as a District Attorney for the State of Massachusetts, Mac would not have thought himself capable of the position he now held.

Twenty-five years ago, he was a completely different man with completely different ideals and a completely different life.

He had been happily married to a wonderful woman. His career was right where he had wanted it to be, and most of all, he thought he was making a difference.

Twenty-five years ago, the name Ken Falco was as anonymous to him as John Doe. The man was simply another grab bag of the seven deadly sins that went into the creation of societies' lowest forms of life. Another one of the many scum who managed to slip though the cracks of the judicial system every year.

Arrested in New York for the rape of two college students, Falco gained his freedom when New York's State Supreme Court ruled the evidence used against him was obtained in an illegal search of his apartment. The scum, feeling he overstayed his welcome in the Big Apple, then migrated to the Bay State. Three months later, he raped and killed the thirty-three year old wife of District Attorney Neil MacGregor.

Life was nothing if not unpredictable.

The days painfully led into weeks that dragged into months. An extended leave of absence from the District Attorney's office and a bottle of whiskey a day couldn't alleviate the pain or the memory of his wife's brutal death. If it wasn't for his chance encounter with Martin West or the recruiting efforts of the Organization, Mac was sure he would have ended his misery in a highly undignified, cowardly manner.

At the time, the Organization was still floundering about, looking for a direction. It was still unaware and unsure of its potential. Only he and Josef Wenzler had the foresight and confidence to forge its destiny, to make a reality of their shared vision. A vision consisting of a Utopian society without drugs, crime or corruption, a society in which people like Ken Falco would be and could be eliminated without any chance of slipping through a loophole. A society in which an army of Alec's, loyal and disciplined, would be the only law, and the Organization the only judge.

He stepped out into the cold air and breathed deeply. The Organization had a noble purpose, and that purpose, above all else, needed to be protected. It was more important than his friendship with Senator Allsworth.

It was more important than his concerns for Alec.

And though he didn't believe it and knew he never would, he forced himself to say it, "More important than Adam."

✶✶✶✶✶✶✶✶✶✶✶✶✶✶✶✶✶✶✶✶✶✶✶✶✶✶✶✶✶✶✶✶✶✶✶✶

Paige took a bite of her tuna fish sandwich and listened to her dinner companion, Peter Jones, as he continued his life story.

"...and my wife and sons were killed in the same accident in which I lost my left arm. I'm afraid I found comfort with the bottle and soon after, I lost my job, my house, and even my self-respect. Before I sobered up, I found myself living in the street, sleeping in a cardboard box or under a bridge or in a doorway. Hard to believe that was almost fifteen years ago."

"You haven't had a drink in eight years though Mr. Jones, that in itself is something to be proud of," Paige offered. "Why haven't you tried getting back into the mainstream of society? You're obviously a very intelligent man."

"Oh my dear, I'm sure you've heard all the excuses before. The truth is, I'm content to live out my days as a street person. God knows I don't have many left. But enough about me, our deal was, in return for me spending the night at your fine establishment, we would discuss your burden. Now tell me about this man who has imprisoned such a lovely heart."

Paige smiled and looked down at her half-eaten sandwich. "It's not his fault. He's in love with somebody else. He's never led me on or given me any reason to believe our relationship was anything but platonic," Paige said sadly, still looking down at her dinner.

"And this man, you're sure he has no other feelings for you other than friendship?"

"Oh, I'm sure. You see it's my older sister he's in love with. They're announcing their engagement this weekend. I tell you, there's no justice in Cupid's court."

"Tell me about him, this man you love. What makes him so special?"

Paige was reluctant at first, almost embarrassed to be discussing such personal matters with a complete stranger. However there was something about Peter Jones that put her at ease. It was that same sense of familiarity she experienced during their initial conversation.

"His name is Adam MacGregor," she began. "He's an attorney for his father's law firm here in town."

And so for the next hour, Paige found herself talking almost non-stop about Adam, almost eager to answer any questions her companion had, and for whatever reason, he had several.

"Paige," one of the volunteers interrupted. "I'm sorry to bother you, but you have a phone call at the front desk."

"Thank you Jane. I'll be right there." Turning to Peter Jones, she excused herself and hurried to the desk. Returning a moment later, she found the table empty.

"Karen," she said to the volunteer at the next table, "did you happen to see where my friend went?"

"He just left Paige. I saw him go out the back door."

Damn. He agreed to spend the night, she thought to herself. It was well below freezing and sure to get colder. Reaching for her coat, she hurried out the back door in hopes of convincing Peter Jones to return with her to the Inn.

A half block from the shelter, she recognized the tweed fedora and the man wearing it as he took a left into a vacant parking lot. Picking up her pace, she made it to the lot just in time to see Peter Jones climbing into the back of a black stretch limousine.

✶✶✶✶✶✶✶✶✶✶✶✶✶✶✶✶✶✶✶✶✶✶✶✶✶✶✶✶✶✶✶✶✶✶✶✶

Placing both palms down on the conference table, Omega stood to address the Board. His face was flushed, and his anger was evident in the tone of his voice.

"Dr. Wenzler has made it perfectly clear the dangers involved with sending Alec on another mission," he began. "But those dangers are minimal and well worth the risk when one considers what's at stake. Unless the Senator is eliminated immediately, there's no telling how many others he shall inform of our Organization. He has already contacted Deputy Director Quinn of the FBI and in the confidence of his lawyer has implied his desire to expose us."

Omega stood at the head of the conference table. Eight members of the Board sat in a semi-circle around him and seven satellite-fed monitors were positioned in the wall to his left. Cigar smoke hung loosely above him like a partially formed poltergeist.

"Why Alec though, Omega? Why not use a field team? Perhaps stage an accident or even a suicide?" asked one of the Board members.

Omega nodded in response to the man's suggestions, acknowledging the idea before speaking again.

"Obviously that would make things easier. However, staging a suicide or even an accident is going to take time. And time is not our ally. As I've stated, Allsworth has already made contact with the FBI.

"We don't know how much the Deputy Director knows or believes at this point. But it's a reasonable assumption that he's put both Allsworth and his house under surveillance. A field team, no matter how covert, runs a great risk of failure. In my opinion, only Alec can get to the Senator quickly and efficiently."

A low murmur of discussion circulated between the members of the Board, as Omega sat down. Sipping his lukewarm coffee, he listened in silence to their hushed debate. He was sure they would come around to his way of thinking. They always did.

Taking longer than Omega expected, it was James Bullings, chief lobbyist of the largest arms supplier to the Pentagon, who finally spoke for the collective group. Addressing Wenzler first, he began solemnly, "Doctor, the Board recognizes your expertise in the field of genetic research and with manipulative brain techniques. Your theory on Alec, though highly speculative, is of great concern. If he is indeed suffering from a memory collapse as you say, then we risk everything seeking to utilize his talents further. But again, what you've told us is only speculation. We're not sure why or what's causing Alec's behavioral problems or his inability to focus his teleportation skills.

The Senator though is a real threat. There's no theory or guesswork involved with the damage he could cause to the Organization."

Turning to face Mac, Bullings continued, "Omega, the majority of the Board agrees with your assessment. We believe that the Senator's decision to betray us is as unfortunate for him as it is for us. We have no alternative but to eliminate him, the sooner the better. The Board approves of your plan to use Alec for this assignment."

"Excellent gentlemen, excellent," Omega said exuberantly. "We'll go over the details later this evening, and Dr. Wenzler and I will begin briefing Alec immediately."

In his relief over the Board's decision, he failed to notice the uneasiness that settled throughout the room.

"Gentlemen, there's no cause for concern," Omega said confidently. "I assure you the Senator's death will in no way be traced back to the Organization."

Again it was Bullings who spoke for the group. "Omega, there is other business which requires our attention. Dr. Wenzler has theorized that if Alec is indeed suffering a memory collapse, there is a very high probability that Adam also is experiencing the same condition. The Board feels that Adam West should be made to undergo reprogramming as well."

Though the words rendered him momentarily speechless, Omega scornfully stared down the length of the table taking in Wenzler's pretentious grin.

"Gentlemen," Omega began in a calm but forceful tone. "Adam West no longer exists. In his place is Adam MacGregor, my son. Dr. Wenzler may or may not have been successful with Alec, only time and further testing will decide. But Adam has never shown the slightest indication of remembering his true past, never mind demonstrating any of the behavioral patterns which Alec is experiencing. There's no basis for the Board's recommendation to have him reprogrammed, and I must strenuously object to the Doctor's unfounded speculation." He finished with a heavy thump of his fist on the table.

The tension in the room grew thicker than the smoke lingering high above the unventilated room. Knowing the Board would never directly oppose Omega, Wenzler was nevertheless satisfied at his rivals loss of composure.

"It's true that I have no concrete evidence that Adam's memory block is collapsing," Wenzler began pompously. "It is *only* a theory. However, I do wish to remind Omega that at one time, Dr. Martin West and his wife also believed young Adam to be beyond reproach. They made the unfortunate mistake of putting *his* interest before the interest of the Organization. For their poor judgment, they paid the ultimate price."

"Are you threatening me?" Omega bellowed, as he took a step toward his antagonist.

Held back by two Board members, Omega struggled for self-control.

"Gentlemen," Bullings hurriedly began, "please, we're all on the same side. We all know and respect Omega's loyalty and devotion to the Organization. If he says Adam is not experiencing any breakthroughs, the Board is satisfied with his word. There will be no immediate action taken against Adam."

Shrugging off the two men still restraining him, Omega gave Wenzler a contemptuous stare and headed for the exit.

"I'll be in my office preparing the details for the Senator's assassination. I'll want Alec briefed and ready to go in a day or two."

****

CHAPTER *Thirteen*

In the dream, Adam stood before an altar in a beautifully decorated church. Wonderfully scented white flowers lined the aisles and black-and-white silk ribbons hung loosely on the seats. He was wearing a black tuxedo, a white winged shirt, black tie, and black shoes.

The church pews were filled with wedding guests Adam had never before met or seen. Rather than the customary suits and formal dresses, the strangers wore white lab jackets and green surgical gowns. And they all had metal clipboards on which they were taking notes.

An organ began to play **Here Comes the Bride**, as Allison began her slow descent down the aisle. Dressed in an all-white wedding gown, complete with a white veil over her face and white gloves stretched to her elbows, she walked gracefully toward him.

Upon reaching the altar, she took his hand in hers, and they both turned to face the minister. Only it wasn't a minister, it was Mac.

In the next instant, Mac was saying, "And with the powers vested in me by the Organization, I pronounce you both the same. You may now kiss the bride, son."

Adam was confused. His head began to spin and his legs felt like jelly. The strangers burst into spontaneous applause, as Adam reluctantly lifted the veil from Allison's face.

Suddenly, her hands gripped his throat, and Adam saw it wasn't Allison, but the look-alike from his previous blackouts. He was forced to his knees, gasping for breath, trying desperately to break the incredibly strong vice grip around his throat. All around him, the reverberations of cheers and applause echoed throughout the church as though he was in some ancient coliseum, with Mac as the emperor. On the verge of passing out, he thought he saw Mac standing above him, thrusting his thumb downward, indicating to his opponent to finish him off.

He woke with a start, still trying to catch his breath and realized he awoke into a different nightmare.

He was curled into the fetal position, completely naked, and in an unfamiliar place. He tried to straighten himself but the area in which he was curled was too small. A thin line of light ran along the floor and Adam saw he was lying on several pairs of shoes.

The closet.

He was lying in his bedroom closet.

As that realization crept over him, a second, equally disturbing, fact became evident.

In his right hand, the plastic grip of a knife was held tightly.

Frantic and terrified, he scurried to find the doorknob and pushed open the closet door.

His bedroom was in shambles. At first, Adam thought somebody had broken into his house, locked him in the closet, then ransacked the place. As terrifying a thought as that was, he preferred it to what he knew had actually happened. He had suffered another episode.

Surveying the bedroom, he noticed his bureau and nightstand were pushed tightly against the door, one on top of the other. The drawers were smashed and lay scattered haphazardly throughout the room. Following his line of sight, he stared in disbelief at the windows. The remaining slabs of wood from the bureau were nailed against the panes, allowing eerie shafts of sunlight to filter through. A hammer and a spilled box of nails lay on the floor beneath the sills.

His mind raced, a thousand questions simultaneously attacking his brain for an explanation. He reasoned that during the blackout, he was terrified someone or something was going to enter his bedroom while he slept. Barricading the door, nailing planks across the window, hiding in the closet, and clutching a knife for protection, had been his way of satisfying that fear.

The muffled ringing of the phone from somewhere beneath the clutter of his bedroom momentarily distracted him from his thoughts. But as he heard his own voice on the answering machine pick up the call, his blood turned to ice.

"He's coming! Help me. He's coming! He's coming! He's coming!" his terrified voice pleaded again and again.

"Adam! Adam are you all right? It's Mac. Pick up the phone."

Still stunned by the message he'd apparently left during his blackout, Adam searched for the phone, finding it under a pile of clothing.

"Mac. Hi." Adam said, trying to sound calm.

"Son, are you all right? What the hell is with that message?" Mac demanded, a little confused and angry at the recording.

"I'm sorry Mac," Adam stammered, trying to think of a plausible excuse. "It was meant as a joke for Paige. I wasn't expecting anyone to call this early."

"Christ son, maybe you should've studied acting rather than law. You had me believing you were really in trouble. Listen, I just wanted to let you know I have a meeting with a computer firm in Waltham this morning. Chances are I'll be tied up a good part of the day. If you need me for anything, just use my beeper."

"All right Mac. No problem," Adam said, still surveying his bedroom. "I'll see you later this afternoon then."

After hanging up the phone, he found his wallet, removed a business card, and dialed the number to Doctor Ronald Leppo's psychiatric office.

✳✳✳✳✳✳✳✳✳✳✳✳✳✳✳✳✳✳✳✳✳✳✳✳✳✳✳✳✳✳✳✳✳✳✳✳✳

It was eight o'clock Tuesday morning when Omega re-entered his office at the Keisler Institute for Genetic Research. He'd left the facility only hours before in an attempt to get some much-needed rest. The effort proved futile however, as he tossed and turned until the arrival of dawn.

Wenzler's parting words of the night before continued to haunt his thoughts.

"Martin West and his wife also believed young Adam to be beyond reproach. They made the unfortunate mistake of putting his interest before that of the Organization."

The not-so-subtle threat forced Omega to relive the memory of a long ago decision. A decision very much like the one he made the night before, a decision that ended the life of a very dear friend.

Only now, after actually being put in the same dilemma as Martin West, was he able to once again respect and admire the man he ordered murdered twenty-three years ago.

If only West's breakthrough strand of DNA hadn't split during pregnancy. If Alec had been the only child as planned, things would have been different. However, to everyone's amazement and disbelief, during the second trimester of Janet West's pregnancy, the embryo did split, and Adam came into being.

At first, it was considered an incredible piece of luck. Identical twins, both with perfected and unlimited biological possibilities. Now they would have two specimens to mold, to experiment with, and to develop.

Alec was born seven minutes ahead of his brother and in the process was the only one to absorb the perfected DNA. Adam did possess higher-than-average intelligence, but the phenomenal breakthroughs in the immune system, nervous system, and parts of the subconscious mind, belonged solely to his older sibling.

It took West and Wenzler more than three years of intense experimentation to determine only Alec was *gifted* in ways that served the Organization.

Though Adam and Alec were physically identical, their personalities were as opposite as good and evil. Adam was responsive, loving, and gentle. He enjoyed being played with, held, and pampered. He had favorite toys that stimulated him on sight. He giggled and cooed upon recognition of his parents and others close to him. In short, he was a happy, normal baby.

Alec though, possessed a certain darkness. He shunned the usual attention given to babies, refusing to be held or coddled. He rarely smiled, showed no interest in toys or games, and most unusual, he never cried.

It wasn't a surprise that Adam quickly became the favorite of the two, and as a result received more love and attention than Alec. It was undoubtedly that disproportionate amount of attention shown to Adam that led Alec to a profound jealousy and a deep-felt hatred for his brother. A hatred which grew daily and which led to two attempts to kill Adam before they were permanently separated. The last time being at the farmhouse in upstate New York.

Adam was easy to love, and unfortunately for his parents, easy to die for.

The experiments on the twins ranged from painful to inhumane, from scientific to sadistic, from educational to pathological.

Through it all though, only Adam suffered.

And suffered greatly.

At the age of three months, both children were given small amounts of poison to ingest. The dosage wasn't enough to kill them, but certainly enough to threaten their lives. Adam became deathly ill. Almost immediately, he became feverish and suffered debilitating cramps along with vomiting and dehydration. Fore more than two days, he passed through various degrees of sickness before finally purging his system of the poison. Alec, on the other hand, never demonstrated the slightest discomfort.

From the time they were six months to a year, they were injected with chicken pox, measles, mumps, and pneumonia. In each episode, Adam not only contracted the disease, but also suffered horribly. On one occasion, an antidote had to be administered to prevent him from dying. With each new test and experiment, Alec showed no signs of infection or distress.

The twins had several small lacerations cut into various parts of their bodies. Adam screamed and cried for hours, and the cuts, some requiring a stitch or two, took the normal time to heal. Alec also bled and showed some pain, but never cried. And unlike his brother, his wound never required stitches, because regardless of their severity, they healed themselves within hours.

The one area Adam did excel and outdistance his brother was in displays of intelligence and rationalization. By the age of two, Adam possessed a vocabulary equal to a child three times his age. He could read and write at a sixth-grade level by the time he was three and was even able to compute basic algebra. The praise he received only fueled his brother's vicious hatred toward him.

Soon after the boys' third birthday, Dr. West and his wife could no longer tolerate the experiments being performed on the children and threatened to go public. They didn't hide the fact it was for Adam's well being they were most concerned.

In hopes of buying time, the Board agreed it was no longer necessary to test Adam. They allowed him to be removed from the lab to more suitable quarters within the facility. It was a result of separating the twins, which led to the amazing discovery of Alec's true abilities.

Realizing his brother no longer shared in the experimentation process, and knowing his own parent's selected Adam over him, Alec's rage soared. One night, as Adam lay sleeping in his new bedroom, Alec simply disappeared from his room and reappeared in Adam's. Caught on cameras mounted in each of the boys' bedrooms, Adam's life was barely saved by the security staff. It was the most phenomenal breakthrough ever imaged. A three-year-old boy with the power of teleportation. If there were a way to control that power, to manipulate it for their own purposes, the possibilities would be unlimited. From those possibilities, the true purpose of the Organization came into being.

A race of superhuman policemen, genetically perfected, physically superior, completely controlled, and totally devoted to the

Organization. Ten years ago, from sperm extracted from Alec, forty-six embryos had been conceived. Nine of the embryos lived through the experimentation process. From the sperm of those nine, the Organization could expect as many as seventy-five more viable clones with equal or greater abilities. And from the sperm of those seventy-five, an infinite number of successes.

By the turn of the millennium, the Organization would be a worldwide force recognized, accepted, and applauded for their control over society. Crime as it was now known would no longer exist. International terrorism, drug trafficking, pornography, wars, and crime-related deaths could be eliminated. The Organization would be the only worldwide authority. No Presidents, no kings or queens, no dictators, only the Organization.

However, Martin West had other plans. He refused to allow any further experiments on either child, and for the good of science and the well being of the children, he tried to go public. He made several calls and on the morning of April 25th, met with two reporters aboard his yacht, Discovery. Shortly after departing, the boat exploded, killing Martin and Janet West, both reporters, and the crew.

Now, twenty-five years later, Omega was faced with the same dilemma as his one-time friend; protect Adam or protect the Organization.

Protect the one and only person he had been able to love unconditionally since his wife's brutal death or protect the Organization and all it stood for.

At nine-fifteen, he locked his office door and made his way through the endless clatter of the monitoring room to meet with Alec and Wenzler. It was the longest walk of his life.

****

Paige pushed her way through the red line subway train, exiting at the Washington Street stop. Like a fish swimming upstream, she fought through the throng of commuters trying to push their way in before she could get out. Finally though, she burst through the underground station into daylight.

She had spent a restless night tossing and turning and was now paying the price. Tired and irritable, she walked briskly the to the homeless shelter.

With each step, the troublesome figure of Peter Jones flashed through her mind.

Why would somebody pretend to be homeless? Somebody who could afford a chauffeured limousine and was obviously intelligent must have better things to do with their time than chat with a social worker.

And what was it about Peter Jones that was so familiar? It certainly wasn't his missing left arm. She was sure she never met anyone without his or her full limbs intact.

It was something else about him, something which continued to elude her.

She tried calling Adam to discuss the strange incident, but his line had been busy from ten o'clock to the time she finally went to bed.

Her mood was only darkened when she assumed he was talking to Allison.

Traffic was sluggish, partly because of the storm the night before and partly due to the morning rush hour. With every slow-moving vehicle, Paige imagined she saw Peter Jones in the passenger seat. With each blare of a horn, she turned quickly, expecting to see his face.

Pulling open the heavy iron doors of the Pine Street Inn, she shook off the cold and stopped at the administration desk.

"Any messages," she asked a volunteer behind the window.

"Good morning Paige. No calls, but this package came for you," she said, holding out what looked like a shoebox wrapped in brown paper.

✶✶✶✶✶✶✶✶✶✶✶✶✶✶✶✶✶✶✶✶✶✶✶✶✶✶✶✶✶✶✶

CHAPTER *Fourteen*

At ten-thirty, Adam stood with his client, David Green, at the Boston Municipal Courthouse. After a lengthy and somewhat heated discussion with the Assistant District Attorney concerning the illegal procedures used to obtain evidence, the State agreed to drop the most serious charges against his client. More as a way of saving face than anything else, the Assistant D.A. held firm on the fifty dollar fine for reckless driving.

The judge reviewed the paperwork handed him by the prosecution and simply shook his head.

"Mr. Green, as to the charge of reckless driving, i.e., failure to use a blinker, how do you plea?"

Green looked at Adam quickly, then boldly answered, "Guilty as charged, your Honor." A slight grin played mischievously across his dark face.

"The court then fines you fifty dollars, Mr. Green. How long will you need to pay?" the judge asked with obvious contempt.

Green turned and scanned the people in the court until his eyes settled on two large bulking white men in very fashionable suits. One had his wallet opened and was counting out five ten-dollar bills.

"If it pleases the court, " Green began, "I can pay it right now," he finished, obviously enjoying his victory over the legal system.

"It would please this court never to see you here again, Mr. Green. Pay the clerk on your way out. Case dismissed," the judge said with a heavy thump of his gavel.

Once outside the stuffy courthouse and on the sleet-covered cobble-stones of the plaza, David Green was met by two beautiful women and one more bodyguard to go with the two in the courthouse. After giving each of the women a kiss and a hug, he turned to Adam and extended his hand.

"One for one, counselor," David said with a wide grin. "I'm having a little celebration at my club this evening and you're the guest of honor," he added, still vigorously shaking Adam's hand.

"I appreciate the offer David, but I have other plans this evening."

"Very well, Adam. But I'm a man who honors his debts and to you I owe an enormous debt of gratitude." Handing Adam a business card, he continued, "I'm a very resourceful individual councilor. Anything you need or want, you come see me first. Pretty good chance I can get it for you below cost, if you get my drift."

With that, David Green climbed into the waiting Cadillac, followed by his entourage, and drove off.

Adam glanced at his watch and noted he still had ninety-minutes until his appointment with Doctor Ronald Leppo. The events of the past two days were beginning to take a heavy toll, both emotionally and physically. He had worked so hard and for so long to get to where he was, it just didn't seem fair life would throw him this kind of curve.

If he was having a nervous breakdown or if his blood tests came back with proof of some brain tumor, why couldn't it had happened years before or preferably many years later?

And why did he have to realize a week before his engagement party he no longer loved Allison? And why, of all people, did he have to fall in love with her sister?

As he got into the cab and it pulled from the curb, the late model Chevy also pulled out into traffic and took the same left turn as the cab.

"I want to thank you again for seeing me on such short notice, Doctor. The Bureau appreciates your cooperation," Thomas said, while showing his identification.

"Well, Agent Thomas I'm just glad our schedules were able to coincide. Now what is it I can assist you with," Doctor Ronald Leppo asked as both men sat down.

Under the pretense of investigating a serial rapist, Thomas had secured an appointment with Leppo to discuss the psychological make-up of potential suspects.

However, his real reason for gaining access to the doctor's office was to plant a small listening device prior to Adam MacGregor's appointment in less than an hour. Thomas planned to be in and out of the office in less than twenty minutes.

"Doctor as I told you on the phone, we have very few physical clues. We're hoping you can shed some light on the type of person we should be focused on."

"I was under the impression the Bureau had staff psychologists for this very reason. Why go outside the Agency?" Leppo asked innocently.

Thomas hated undercover work, instead preferring the straightforward surveillance or hard-nosed interrogations. Doctor Leppo was a perfect example as to why. Too many questions requiring him to think fast on his feet, something he hated whether on his feet, his ass, or his back.

"Well Doctor," Thomas began slowly. "The truth is…well, the truth is I'm not at liberty to reveal that information."

That usually worked.

"Agent Thomas, I don't wish to appear uncooperative, but there are confidentiality laws in this state. If you suspect one of my patients or are in any way attempting to solicit information protected by those confidentiality laws, I'm afraid I'm going to have to ask you to leave."

It usually worked, but not always.

"Doctor, I assure you, the Bureau is well aware of any state or local laws in may come in conflict with. I respect your professionalism as

well as your position. I hope you can respect mine. The Bureau is neither interested in nor suspicious of any of your patients. I'm here
only as a law enforcement agent attempting to put together a psychological profile of a serial rapist. We believe this person is responsible
for at least fifteen rapes in three states. Any help you can offer will be
greatly appreciated."

There, that should do it.

"I'm curious Agent Thomas, how did the Bureau happen to stumble
upon my practice, if I may ask?"

*Christ this guy didn't quit. How would you like me to stumble over your
face you Goddamn piece of…?*

"Doctor, please. If you're uncomfortable with aiding in our investigation or feel for any reason the Bureau has a false curriculum in soliciting
your opinion, I'd be glad to terminate our interview."

Right after I terminate you!

"I apologize for putting you through the third degree, so to speak,
Agent Thomas. It's just this day and age, one can never be too careful
about what he says or does. Please, just give me a few minutes to review
the file you brought and I'll be happy to give you a profile."

As the doctor opened the manila file containing information about a
phony rapist in a phony investigation, Thomas casually strolled to the
window opposite the desk. Turning to lean against the sill and to keep
an eye on the doctor, he carefully slid the satellite-powered listening
device under the clapboard of the window.

Alec lay motionless, almost catatonic, in the neurological lab. The
bed on which he rested electronically monitored his vital statistics and
recorded them overhead onto three digital screens. As before, a set of
headphones played a varied selection of music intertwined with subliminal messages and a pair of virtual reality glasses were strapped
tightly to his head.

Omega sat with Wenzler and two technicians on the opposite side of
the one-way mirror. The technicians, aware of the hostilities between
the two most powerful men within the Organization, did their best to
keep preoccupied.

Omega leaned closer, fogging the mirror with his breath, and studied
Alec for any sign of potential problems. Satisfied with what he saw, he
leaned back and turned to Wenzler.

"How much longer?" he asked.

Wenzler continued scribbling notes, apparently seeing fit to answer
his superior when ready.

"Eighteen to twenty-four hours," he said finally without looking up
from his chart.

Omega nodded thoughtfully, silently calculating the stringent time
frame in which they had to work. He glanced at the technicians busy
with their work, then turned to Wenzler.

"I wonder if I may have a word with you in private, Doctor," Omega
asked, rising from his seat.

Wenzler sighed heavily, letting it be known he resented the interrup-
tion, then gestured toward the door. "After the bluegrass, go directly
into the big band era, then country," he said to one of the technicians.
"If he shows any signs of agitation, get me immediately."

"The music is new. Why?" Omega asked once the door closed
behind them.

"Why not? Music is, after all, the universal language of man and I've
found it to have a soothing effect on his subconscious mind. Alec
responds well to several types of music. I'm looking for the one he
responds to best."

"But why now? This could very well be his most important mission
and probably his last for an unspecified period of time. Don't you think
the timing is a little risky?" Omega asked.

"Personally, I think this whole damn mission is a little risky, Omega.
But the Board seemed to feel your concerns slightly outweighed mine,"

Wenzler said in a harsh whisper. "If we have to send Alec out, I want to take whatever precautions I can to keep his rage under control and bring him back in relatively the same condition as he leaves. Of course, if you feel my procedures are as unfounded as my theories, you're more than welcome to convene the Board and discuss your own alternative," he added with contempt.

"That won't be necessary Doctor, but I do expect Alec to be ready to go by tomorrow afternoon," Omega said. "After that the Allsworth home will be crawling with extra security and staff in preparation for Saturday night's party."

Wenzler shook his head with a contemptible smirk. "It seems a pity to ruin young Adam's engagement party, doesn't it?" he said smugly. "But then again, we all have to make sacrifices for the Organization, don't we?" he asked rhetorically.

"Tomorrow afternoon, Doctor. I want Alec ready by then," Omega said, refusing to be drawn into Wenzler's trap.

"We all need to make sacrifices for the Organization, Omega," Wenzler said one more time as his nemesis walked away.

CHAPTER *Fifteen*

For the remainder of the morning, Adam kept himself preoccupied with paperwork and research. At one o'clock, not wanting to risk another episode, he hailed a cab outside the law firm.

"209 Madison Avenue, Brookline," he said absently to the driver.

The Brookline office of Doctor Leppo was no more than a twenty minute drive, but with the lunch hour commute and traffic still sluggish from the previous night's snowstorm, Adam knew it would be closer to an hour.

During his ride through the congested streets of Boston, he stared silently out the grime-covered window of the taxi. Neither the occasional static from the dispatcher nor the country music playing softly from the cabbie's portable radio were able to penetrate his thoughts.

"What the hell's happening to me?" he asked for the hundredth time that morning.

And for the hundredth time, there was no answer.

Arriving at his destination with ten minutes to spare, he gave the cabby a twenty-dollar bill for a twelve-dollar fare and pensively made his way into the medical building. The directory listed three floors and a Doctor Ronald Leppo in Suite 312.

He rode the elevator alone, still lost in thought, and exited onto the third floor. Walking slowly, he passed the offices of a small law firm, a temp service and a chiropractor, before finally coming to Suite 312. In small stenciled lettering, the door read, **Doctor R nald Leppo.** The 'o' had peeled off some time ago and Adam wondered if the doctor was too busy to replace it or just too lazy to care. Pulling open the door, he was relieved to see an empty waiting room with the exception of a secretary sorting through the day's mail.

"Krystal, I presume," Adam asked casually as they made eye contact.

The secretary looked surprised, but smiled nevertheless. "Yes, I am. And you are?" she asked pleasantly.

"Adam MacGregor. We spoke briefly on the phone this morning."

"Of course. Good afternoon Mr. MacGregor. I trust you had no trouble finding us."

"No problem at all," he replied, hoping his nervousness wasn't as transparent as it felt.

"Good. Dr. Leppo is still with a patient, but if you wouldn't mind filling out this form, I'm sure he'll be with you shortly."

He took the two-page document and a pen from the secretary and sat in the chair furthest from her desk.

He wondered what type of madness she encountered on a daily basis.

Would she find his bizarre behavior boring compared to others who sought out the doctor's help?

Was his condition as common as the flu or as exotic as the plague?

He wondered how long she worked in this environment, whether she was married, had any children, or maybe a pet. He wondered about the moons circling Jupiter and the cosmic force that drew canines to fire hydrants. Anything that distracted him from why he was sitting in a psychiatrist's office was worthy of contemplation.

Just as he finished the form, a middle-aged man, very much overweight and very nervous, exited the doctor's office wearing a three-piece suit, brown loafers, a surgical mask over his face, and rubber gloves on his hands.

Please don't be Dr. Leppo, Adam thought.

"Next Friday at three o'clock then Mr. Elliot," a second man said from just inside the doorway.

"Thank you Doctor. Until then," the synthetically protected man said.

He eyed Adam suspiciously on his way to the door, pausing only a second, before tuning to the secretary.

"Good day, Krystal," he said, bowing his head slightly.

"Good day, Mr. Elliot."

Probably a judge, Adam mused.

"Mr. MacGregor," Doctor Leppo said, as he approached from his office.

Adam was slightly surprised by the appearance of the boyish man standing before him. He was well-built, with a head of thick, wavy black hair, sparkling gray eyes, a friendly smile, and no noticeable stubble on his solidly sculptured face. He looked younger than Adam, but had a certain maturity that comes with years of a practiced bedside manner.

"Hi," was all Adam could think to say, standing to shake the man's hand.

"Shall we step inside the office and get to know each other?" the doctor suggested in his best, *just relax everything's going to be O.K.,* voice.

****

Bathed in an abundance of unnatural yellow lighting, Alec laid motionless in the neurological examination room. He was somewhere he didn't want to be, somewhere between consciousness and his own private hell. It was a place he had no control and a darkness from which he had no escape.

He had been successful in his assassination of Santiago, but his insatiable anger and his need to serve it had clung desperately to his soul and teleported back with him. He knew he killed at least two members of the Organization upon his return. It was an act that was sure to enrage his handlers and sure to place even further doubts into their minds.

In his semi-catatonic state, it seemed every sound echoed a hundred times louder upon entering his eardrums. The oxygen-rich air escaping through the nasal inserts hissed menacingly, as though he were lying helpless in a pit of snakes. The constant hum of the overhead monitors reverberated violently throughout his body and the rhythmic beeping of the heart monitor continued to send painful jabs into his ears with each beat. And though it made no sound, he imagined the intravenous line inserted in a vein behind his left wrist, crashed into him like an unrelenting waterfall with each drip. The metallic, astringent odors of antiseptics became increasingly noxious and left a bitter taste in his dry, parched mouth.

And through it all, he knew they were watching him.

Omega, Wenzler, technicians, Board members, they were always watching him.

Always waiting for the slightest indication of a potential problem. They were never satisfied or content. Always wanting and expecting more from him. Always expecting him to be more like...like someone or something he couldn't remember. Though he was close, the flirting memory passed by like a spring breeze, momentarily satisfying, but leaving him longing for more.

A name.

A face.

They passed each other like speeding trains into opposite ends of a tunnel. Colliding together to make one, but always just beyond his sight.

A thunderous boom, followed by another and another, jolted his thoughts. Closer and louder the crescendo approached.

Footsteps.

Footsteps amplified a thousand times, resounding like a sonic boom inside his head.

He grimaced inwardly as the syringe plunged deep into his right arm. It was the second or third time, he had been injected. He couldn't remember.

A feeling of warmth overcame him in seconds.

The drug was used to relax him and make him feel less angry, less violent, and easier to control. He knew this, and it only made him angrier, more violent, and more determined to remember what he has been made to forget.

He tried to fight the effect of the drug, but the damn music countered his concentration. He was determined to remember this time. Determined to know both the name and face of his private demon, and determined to remember the how and why of his hatred toward him.

As strong as his desire was though, it was no match for the drug, and soon he passed into a deep sleep. A sleep haunted by nightmares of a past they have stolen.

✷✷✷✷✷✷✷✷✷✷✷✷✷✷✷✷✷✷✷✷✷✷✷✷✷✷✷✷✷✷✷✷✷✷✷✷

Her wide brown eyes, as dark as chocolate and just as sweet, couldn't possibly understand the seriousness of the situation.

As Tanisha Caroll listened with feigned interest, Paige stood before the three-person panel and gave her opinion as to why the Department of Social Services should not separate the four-year-old child from her biological mother.

Her mother, nineteen-year-old Rita Carroll, had been a prostitute, drug addict, and petty thief since before her teen years. In the last six months though, as a resident of the Inn, she had been drug-free and working as a waitress at a local coffee shop. During that span, Tanisha had been living with a foster family in Boston.

With letters of recommendation and support from the staff, Rita's priest, and her employer, Paige presented what she felt was a strong case for the Carroll family unit.

The decision of the Board would not be made until the end of the week, and after dropping Rita off at work and Tanisha off at the Inn's day care center, Paige returned to her office.

The off-white walls, with its permanent layer of gray dust and low ceilings, only confirmed the feelings of dread and confusion she felt earlier that morning. Reaching into the lower left-hand drawer of her metal desk, she removed the package that had been delivered to her upon her arrival.

The shoebox had no return address or note indicating the sender and just as strange were the photographs contained within.

Twenty or so black and white pictures of twin boys at various stages of childhood, a couple of photos of a beautiful farmhouse, a map of upstate New York and two or three pictures of a man and woman posing aboard a yacht named Discovery. Most disturbing though was a color photo of her and Adam at a concert they attended last year at the Boston Common.

What they had in common, Paige couldn't begin to fathom. Who sent them and why, was just as baffling.

However, there was one thing she was sure of. Though he was about twenty years younger and had both arms, the man aboard the yacht was definitely Peter Jones.

✶✶✶✶✶✶✶✶✶✶✶✶✶✶✶✶✶✶✶✶✶✶✶✶✶✶✶✶✶✶✶✶✶✶✶✶

"It's almost two o'clock Bob," Gloria Allsworth announced to her husband through the closed door of his study. "The photographer will be here in less than an hour," she said with a flare of concern.

The Senator, as he had on the last two occasions his wife updated him on the time, continued transcribing what he knew of the Organization, including names, addresses and dates.

An aide from his office would be arriving shortly to hand deliver a copy of the memo to his youngest daughter at the Pine Street Inn and the original to Mac's law firm in Boston.

He finished the fourth page of names, now totaling one hundred and twenty-four, sat back, took a long sip of scotch, and thought hard about what to write next.

He had to make the unbelievable sound real, the impossible sound plausible, and the unimaginable sound feasible. He somehow had to convey to Quinn the reality of the genetic breakthrough accomplished by Doctor Martin West before his death. He had to make him aware of the depth of the Organization and of the power they possessed.

Draining the last of the scotch from his glass, he rose from his leather high-back chair and walked thoughtfully to the bar. The liquor was bringing his own mortality into focus, and as he filled the glass with fresh scotch and two ice cubes, a life-long list of regrets began passing through his clouded thoughts.

The one that seemed to anchor the others was the emotional void between father and daughter, between flesh and blood, between him and Paige.

How foolish he had been not to realize how special and different she was from Allison. How blind not to see a younger, more idealistic version of himself in his daughter. The years that he wasted trying to force Paige into a mold he felt best suited his political aspirations were gone. Trying to fit her into a personality that only compromised her beliefs and convictions had succeeded in only causing a deep rift in their relationship. What should have been the happiest times of his life were filled only with memories of crying, arguing, threats, and tears.

And now, with his entire world crumbling around him, he realized the only other person he could trust was the one person he constantly pushed away. The one person who had always been second to Allison.

Sitting down behind his desk again, the Senator put aside the memo on the Organization and took out a blank piece of letterhead.

Suddenly it became more important to let Paige know of his shortcomings and to ask her forgiveness than it was to finish his revelations about the Organization.

✶✶✶✶✶✶✶✶✶✶✶✶✶✶✶✶✶✶✶✶✶✶✶✶✶✶✶✶✶✶✶✶✶✶✶

Chapter *Sixteen*

The music continually interrupted his thoughts, and the virtual reality goggles made it almost impossible to focus on anything other than the desired scenario of the Organization. Nevertheless, bits and pieces of a past long ago erased managed to filter through.

He was remembering, and with each fragment of recall came a surge of hope and anger.

He could remember a happier time, a time when he was something more than a pawn for Omega and Wenzler. A time when he was loved by someone for who he was and not because of what he was. A time long ago as a child when...when what?

Something happened that caused him to be a prisoner in this dark world. Someone had to be responsible for the void in his memory and in his heart.

An image of a woman, beautiful and full of love, flickered briefly through his thoughts.

She was holding him, telling him how wonderful he was and how much she loved him.

His mother?

Maybe. Yes, definitely. It was his mother.

But where was she now when he needed her most? When he so desperately needed to hear those words and feel that love and compassion. Where was she in his darkest hour?

Then a horrific memory flashed before his thoughts. It wasn't him she was holding. It was the Other!

The Imposter!

The Look-alike!

It was him. He was the one responsible for stealing his childhood, his parents, and his freedom.

Yes, it was coming back now. The Imposter, failing at every experiment, always sick, always in pain and always crying. Yet somehow, always the one his parents and the Organization praised and comforted.

Yes, the Imposter had been able to fool everyone around him. He had been able to somehow convince the Organization he was better, stronger, and more worthy of their affection.

The Imposter was a threat. Alec knew it before anyone else. He had not been fooled. That was why he tried to kill him when they were children, and that was why he would try to kill him once again. By eliminating the threat he could prove to the Organization it was he who was worthy of their love.

The sharp pain in his left arm lasted only a second and he knew he had been injected once again with a drug that was designed to send him back to his own private hell. This time though it would be different.

As he drifted out of consciousness, he knew he would awake with memories of the Imposter intact.

Parked on the Washington Street side of the homeless shelter, Adam waited nervously for Paige. It was just after four-thirty when he called her from his cell phone to confirm they were still on for dinner.

"Of course we are, Adam," Paige replied eagerly.

"Good, I have something very important to discuss with you," he told her. And regardless of her prompting, he refused to go into details until dinner.

As he sat and waited, he could feel his courage begin to wane. The ninety-minute session with Doctor Leppo had given Adam the conviction needed to tell Paige of his true feelings about her and Allison.

Hesitant at first, the doctor's professional approach and friendly demeanor had eventually gotten to Adam. He openly began discussing his reasons for the appointment and honestly and eagerly answered any questions the doctor may have had, regardless of how personal.

There were questions about his childhood before the adoption, to which Adam had no recollection, questions about his grandmother and the farmhouse in his visions, and very personal questions about his feelings toward Allison and Paige. Finally, toward the end of their session, Adam listened intently to the doctor's opinions.

"From what we have been able to establish today Adam, and I caution you, this is only a preliminary opinion, I have two suggested prognosis for your strange behavior," he began, flipping back to the beginning of his notes.

"The first and probably the most logical explanation is simply an exaggerated case of anxiety. It's not that uncommon, especially in young people. You've just experienced perhaps the most stressful three years of your life at law school. Coupled with the intense studying you did for the bar, the pressures of living up to your father's expectations and legacy, along with the stress related to your pending break-up, the only thing that surprises me is it didn't happen sooner.

"It doesn't mean you're ready for a straight jacket or a padded room. What it does mean though is you need to learn the proper ways to vent the inevitable stress life brings in a more open, positive way. I'm certainly not advocating the break-up with," he paused briefly to check his notes, "Ms. Allsworth. However, if that is *your* intention, I highly recommend you do it immediately. The anxiety it's causing will only get worse the longer you allow it to fester."

"But what about the memory flashes, the blackouts, and the message I wrote on my bedroom mirror," Adam pointed out. "There's nothing extraordinary about them?"

"Well to be honest Adam, they're quite extraordinary. And that leads me to my second possibility for your behavior."

"Which is?" Adam asked hesitantly.

"You may be suffering from fugues."

"Sounds fatal," Adam said only half-joking.

"With the proper psychological counseling, they're not even painful," Doctor Leppo replied in the same joking tone Adam had used. "You see, a fugue is a serious personality dissociation. A person who suffers from this condition can go places, talk to people, they can engage in just about any activity all the while giving the impression of normalcy. Later though, this person is unable to recall where he has been, who he has seen or talked to, or what has transpired during this period. It's as though the time frame in question passed while he was in a deep sleep."

Adam was silent for a moment, staring thoughtfully at his bandaged hand. "I have no memory of those twenty-eight minutes yesterday morning. I got dressed, went to the kitchen, retrieved a knife, sliced my hand and left a rather ambiguous message on my mirror. And I certainly don't have any memory of turning my bedroom into a fortress last night. For Christ sakes, I nailed my windows shut. Those things sound as though they fall into the second category you described. Is twenty-eight minutes a long time to experience a fugue?" he asked.

"There's no time limit on how long they can last. A fugue could be a few minutes, a few hours, even a few days, and yes those two incidents do sound like you suffered through a fugue."

"But you're pretty sure it was only an anxiety attack, right?" Adam asked hopefully.

"Fugues are usually brought on by repressed memories. Usually physical or sexual abuse, traumas, witnessing a horribly frightening ordeal, just about anything the subconscious mind feels it can't deal with. Over time, those memories begin to surface, usually involuntarily. Psychologically, the subconscious isn't ready to reveal its secrets and as a result forces the conscious mind to blackout.

"During our interview, I asked you several questions regarding your childhood and those involved with it. Again I caution you, it was only a preliminary interview, but I didn't hear or sense anything that would alert me to any hidden trauma. What I suggest is some spring cleaning for the soul. If there are issues in your life causing you unusual amounts of stress and anxiety, deal with them immediately. Relax a little and enjoy what you've accomplished. After you've done an honest inventory of your life, and after you've taken care of the issues that need taking care of, then I'd like to see you again. If however, you experience any more blackouts or strange episodes, I'd like to see you immediately. Perhaps there are certain things in your past you're not even aware of which could be causing your condition. In which case, I would suggest regressive therapy."

"Regressive therapy? What exactly does that consist of?" Adam asked.

"Nothing you don't want it to. Normally we'll discuss you're life in chronological order from the present backwards. If we come across any gaps or discrepancies about certain areas, more than likely we've found the key to your behavior."

After Adam left the office of Doctor Leppo, he was confident once he told Paige and Allison how he felt, things would return to some semblance of normalcy. However, waiting outside the Inn for Paige, he began to have his doubts.

A homeless man struggled to push a shopping cart full of possessions through the unshoveled snow on the sidewalk across the street from Adam's car. The man stopped briefly, looked around as though he was being followed, then laughed loud enough for Adam to hear through his closed window.

The poor soul probably suffered anxiety attacks when he was younger too, Adam thought. *Probably never gave his soul a good spring-cleaning. Probably married someone he didn't love. Probably lived his whole life loving someone else but never had the courage to tell her. Probably never even...*

The rapping on his passenger side window startled him momentarily. He wasn't sure if his increased heartbeat was from being startled or from seeing Paige peer in through the window. He unlocked the door and pushed it open for her.

"I'm sorry," she said sincerely. "Were you waiting long?"

"Not long at all," he lied. "Are you hungry?"

"Starving. I had such a hectic day I worked straight through lunch," she answered.

For a split second, Adam had to fight the compulsion to lean over the console and kiss her. A long, soft, *I Love You* kiss that would convey to her everything he hoped to say over dinner.

"I took the liberty of using Mac's clout to get us reservations at Giovanni's in the North End. I hope you're in the mood for Italian," he said.

"Giovanni's. Oh Adam, I'm not dressed up enough to go there. I didn't even put on make-up."

She must be the only one in the world not to realize how beautiful she is, Adam thought.

"Paige, I bet you'll be the prettiest woman there, with or without make-up."

"Oh my," she responded playfully. "Your second day as an attorney and already you've learned how to B.S. your way past a jury. Giovanni's it is then," she said as they both laughed.

✶✶✶✶✶✶✶✶✶✶✶✶✶✶✶✶✶✶✶✶✶✶✶✶✶✶✶✶✶✶✶✶✶✶

Chapter *Seventeen*

"Do you still think the Senator's death can wait?" Omega asked, as Wenzler flipped through the list of names in front of him.

An aide from Allsworth's office delivered a copy of the memo about an hour ago to Mac's office. He now shared the damaging evidence with Wenzler and two other members of the Board.

"This is incredible," one of the members said slowly. "How does he know so much about us? We've pretty much kept him in the dark about most of our operation."

"Gentlemen, he's been a member for almost twenty-five years. He's not blind. Doctor, I want Alec ready to go in a couple of hours," Omega said firmly.

"Twelve hours, minimum," Wenzler said without taking his eyes from the document.

"Doctor, perhaps you overlooked the fact that your name is the first one listed on the Senator's memo. Or perhaps it was the Senator's accurate portrayal of what our Organization stands for and the meticulous descriptions of what we're capable of accomplishing that went unnoticed. Either way Doctor, I'm not asking, I'm ordering. I want Alec prepped and ready in two hours. Is that understood?"

"I can't guarantee that Alec will respond to...."

"Doctor, you can't seem to guarantee much of anything lately!" Omega said harshly. "But let me tell you what *I* can guarantee. I can guarantee that unless the Senator is eliminated this evening, before any more information about our Organization becomes public knowledge, we'll be lucky if we're able to continue this debate behind bars. Now you get him ready or I'll find someone who can!"

Followed by the two Board members, Omega slammed the door behind him, leaving Wenzler to fume in private.

✱✱✱✱✱✱✱✱✱✱✱✱✱✱✱✱✱✱✱✱✱✱✱✱✱✱✱✱✱✱✱✱✱✱✱✱

The drive from the Pine street Inn to Giovanni's Restaurant in the North End was slow and sluggish. The City imposed parking bans on most of the one-way streets, and it took Adam an additional twenty minutes to find a spot. The maitre d', dressed in an Armani lookalike, greeted them at the reservation desk and led them to their table.

"Enjoy your dinner," he said with a fake accent, as he pushed in Paige's chair. "Your waiter this evening shall be Antonio."

The table was covered with a red silk cloth. Two unlit candles stood erect in fine pewter candleholders, and a leather-bound wine list lay in the center. As always, Giovanni's was crowded, but maintained a quiet, well-groomed ambiance. The walls were covered with a wet red silk fabric, and violin music pulsed from somewhere within them. Soft fluorescent lighting cast a romantic shade throughout the authentic Italian décor. Adam couldn't have hoped for a better setting.

"Well, Mr. Attorney," Paige began, "on the phone you said you had something important to discuss with me. I must warn you though, my legalese consists of old Perry Mason reruns," she said with a smile.

I love you, Paige. Four words, that's all. Just say it and be done with it, Adam tried prodding himself. *I love you, just say it.*

"Paige, I hope this doesn't ruin what we have together but," Adam took a breath before continuing. Paige, I…."

"Would you like to order cocktails before dinner or perhaps something from our wine list?" Antonio said from behind Adam's shoulder.

"Oh, the day I've had, I'd love a glass of white wine, please," Paige answered.

The day you've had, I'm still having, Adam thought.

"Rolling Rock in a glass, please," Adam said with an icy stare.

"Very good," Antonio said, not bothering to write it down. He handed them each a menu and left with the wine list.

"Anyway, as I was saying. What I have to tell you may come as a shock and it may change the way you feel about our relationship, but believe me, I've given it a great deal of thought," he began again.

"Adam, if it makes it any easier, whatever you have to say, I promise it's not going to affect the way I feel about you or our friendship," Paige said, feeling a bit uneasy toward Adam's tone.

"It doesn't make it any easier, but thank you for trying. As a matter of fact, there's really no easy way to say it, so I might as well just blurt it out. Paige," he paused to gain a last bit of courage. Before he could continue, Antonio was back, this time to light the candles on the table.

The waiter struck the match and immediately the flame penetrated Adam's conscious thoughts.

HE'S COMING!

"No, not now," Adam said loudly, without realizing he spoke the words.

"I'm sorry sir. Would you prefer not to dine by candlelight this evening?" Antonio asked, surprised at the request.

Adam knew the restaurant was crowded, but the faces, and the voices connected to them, began to melt from view.

"Adam," Paige said. "Adam, what is it? What's wrong?"

HE'S COMING!

The flame from the match was now the only thing he was able to focus on, and suddenly, it was no longer a match. It was the farmhouse. He was surrounded by flames and heat, the smoke choking his lungs, as he tried to get closer to the building. He didn't want to look up toward the attic, but he was no longer in control. From the small octagon-shaped window he could see himself smiling down from above.

HE'S COMING!

"Adam, stop it. What are you doing?"

He recognized Paige's worried voice, but it wasn't enough to pull him back. Instead, it propelled him into a different nightmare, a different place. He and his lookalike, as toddlers, maybe two or three years old, were being injected with a syringe. They were strapped to a metal gurney. He was crying hysterically, but the lookalike simply stared at him and smiled that awful smile. It was as though he enjoyed the fear and terror that emanated from the gurney next to his.

Faces of complete strangers watched from behind a plate glass window. The words, *pneumonia virus* and *should die within twenty-four hours*, echoed the room.

"He's coming. He's going to kill me," Adam yelled. The terrifying vision suddenly merged itself with reality. Two men were trying to restrain him, but his fear was stronger than their hold. Breaking free, he sprinted for the door, knocking over a table and the maitre d' on the way.

****

CHAPTER *Eighteen*

"He's ready," said a technician standing directly behind Wenzler.

The Doctor glanced sideways at Omega for a moment, then said in an uncharacteristically soft voice, "Go ahead Alec."

A second later, Alec was gone.

When he opened his eyes, he was standing next to the wet bar in the Senator's private study. Fifteen feet in front of him, the Senator sat behind an antique oak desk, his head resting between his hands, a glass of scotch to his left.

A slight grin played across Alec's mouth, as he realized he transported on target. Instinctively, he felt for the 9mm automatic, equipped with a silencer, tucked under his belt.

The movement caught the Senator's attention, and he glanced up quickly, unable to hide the surprise in his eyes.

"Adam, my boy. You startled me. I didn't hear you come in," the Senator said quickly.

That name.

Adam.

Alec felt momentarily disorientated, but quickly regained his composure.

"Good evening Senator. I've come to deliver you a message."

"A message? From Mac?" he asked, confused by the statement.

"Mac?" No, I don't know anybody named Mac. My message is from the Organization."

The Senator had begun to rise from his chair, but upon mention of the Organization, he fell heavily into the seat.

"Organization? What Organization, Adam? I'm afraid I'm a little confused," he said with a slight tremble to his voice.

That name again.

Adam. Adam who?

I should know that name, Alec thought.

"Come, come now Senator," Alec taunted, trying to stay focused. "The Organization you're trying to destroy." Glancing quickly at his wristwatch, he noted sadly that he had only fifteen seconds till recall. "I wish there were more time to play this game, Senator, but unfortunately, time is something neither of us has much of," he said coldly, while removing the pistol from his belt.

Before the Senator could scream for help or shield his body, two bullets pierced his chest and a third drilled his forehead.

"Sleep tight Senator," Alec said, as he slowly approached the slumped body.

With eight seconds till recall, Alec casually scanned his handiwork and the desk on which the body slumped. He held the limp left wrist of Allsworth between two fingers, letting it fall to the desk when he was sure there was no pulse.

Then with only two seconds till recall, he saw it.

The 8 x 10 portrait of Adam and Allison standing in a garden.

In that split second, the dam that had been holding back his suppressed memories gave way with a fury.

Anger, rage, and hatred, all at once, surged to the forefront of his consciousness. All the years of trying to remember, searching for a name and a face to his private tormentor had come to rest.

The Lookalike was alive and well. So close Alec could almost touch him.

Soon though, he would be dead and buried.

Raising both arms, as if a victor in some heavyweight bout, Alec let out a triumphant shriek, then vanished.

✳✳✳✳✳✳✳✳✳✳✳✳✳✳✳✳✳✳✳✳✳✳✳✳✳✳✳✳✳✳✳✳✳✳✳

"Where the hell is he?" Omega bellowed, his face reddened with anger. "Where is Alec?"

Wenzler, too, was angry. He knew what happened. Alec should have returned twenty seconds ago, but was still missing. With an accusatory finger pointed at Omega, his voice loud and filled with hostility, Wenzler shouted back; "I told you he wasn't ready. I warned you the mission was too risky. Somehow he has been able to override the recall. He's gone."

CHAPTER *Nineteen*

Adam's nostrils were assaulted by the putrid stench of dried urine on concrete flooring, and his ears took similar punishment from the drunk lying beside him, slurring the words to *Moon River*.

The familiar throbbing sensation, which seemed to have a permanent residence behind his left eye, thumped in unison to the off-key lyrics.

At first he thought he was experiencing another fugue and quickly scrambled off the floor, pressing his back against a set of iron bars. In addition to the singing drunk, two other men occupied space in the small caged room, both curled in the fetal position, mumbling incoherently in their sleep.

To his complete bewilderment, he realized it wasn't a fugue that held him prisoner this time, but a local jail cell. He lowered himself slowly to the floor trying to remember the sequence of events that led him to his current predicament.

He remembered dinner at Giovanni's or at least part of the dinner.

Paige was with him, he could remember that.

They ordered drinks, he could remember that.

The damn waiter had chosen the most inopportune moments to offer his services, he could remember that.

But nothing else.

He tried in vain to recall what led him to his detainment in a holding cell. What crime was he capable of during a fugue? What sort of Mr. Hyde did he become when Dr. Jeckyl wasn't around? Suddenly, he didn't want to know.

He checked his watch, but discovered it was missing, along with his tie, shoelaces, and wallet.

Standard procedure, Adam thought.

As the drunk went into a chorus from **Man of La Mancha**, Adam strained to hear the other voices emanating from just beyond the cell. The wonderfully scented aroma of fresh brewed coffee also found its way down the corridor.

"MacGregor, Adam," a voice bellowed from just beyond his sight. An officer approached the cell, holding a doughnut in one hand and a cup of coffee in the other. A stomach the size of an overripe melon stretched the uniform to its maximum capacity and jiggled uncontrollably with each corpulent step. A patch on his right sleeve said Barnstable Police Department.

At least he knew where he was. Some seventy miles from where he last remembered being.

"I see you've finally slept it off," the guard said without looking at him. Holding the doughnut between his teeth, he fumbled for the right key on an over-filled ring. Unlocking the cell door, he motioned for Adam to follow.

"Was I arrested for something?" Adam asked hesitantly.

"Nah, you were arrested for no reason at all. It was a pretty slow night, so me and the boys thought it might be fun to round up some honest law-abiding citizens for a change," the guard said, his gut bouncing in sync with his chuckle. "Hope it wasn't too much of an inconvenience," he added.

"I'm a lawyer," Adam replied in hopes of getting some answers.

"Well, so much for arresting honest law-abiding citizens. You should have dropped a couple of business cards back there on the floor. I'm sure those boys will need a lawyer soon enough," the guard said with a mouthful of doughnut.

"Where are we going?" Adam asked, too tired and confused to argue.

"Your bails been posted. I don't know about you, but I'm calling it a day. Since you're bonded, I guess you can do whatever you want."

Again the guard fumbled with his key-chain, then slid open a heavy iron door leading to the front of the police station.

Sunlight glared in through a large ox-bow window causing Adam to squint and shield his eyes. At some point during his fugue, morning leapfrogged the night. How many nights and which morning it was though, he couldn't be sure.

"MacGregor, Adam," the guard said to the officer behind the desk. "Hope you enjoyed your stay," he said, as he walked off, his stomach a good five or six inches in front.

The desk sergeant was a middle-aged man, bald as an egg, but built like a tank. He reached behind his chair and grabbed a manila envelope, pouring its contents onto the desk. Adam's wallet, watch, shoelaces, tie, belt, car keys, and some change, tumbled forth.

"Check your belongings and sign the release form. You have a court date two weeks from Monday," he said in a non-caring tone.

"Can I get a copy of the arresting officer's report, please? I'm an attorney," Adam asked in a forced politeness.

The sergeant raised his eyes just high enough to meet Adam's and nodded. Adam wasn't sure if he saw contempt or sympathy in his stare. A minute or two later he read a list of charges brought against him; speeding, resisting arrest, driving to endanger, and assaulting a police officer. Shaking his head in disbelief, Adam looked around the empty station house and asked, "Who posted my bail?"

"Didn't want to leave his name," the desk sergeant answered. "He said he was a friend of yours, paid five hundred dollars cash, signed the bail receipt as John Doe, then left."

Just when he thought things couldn't get any stranger.

"Do you remember what he looked like?" Adam asked, hoping the sergeant was in a more cooperative mood than the guard.

"Older gentleman, grayish white hair, brown overcoat, tweed fedora, and he was missing his left arm."

"His left arm?" Adam said more as a statement than a question. "Did he leave a number or address where he could be reached?"

The sergeant gave him a wry grin and said, "What, you have more than one friend missing a left arm?"

Before he could answer, a familiar voice sounded from the opposite end of the jail.

"Adam, thank God you're all right. I got here as soon as I could," Paige said, as she ran to him.

****

"He's coming. He wants to kill me. Let me go, please, you've got to let me go," the high-pitched, terrified voice pleaded.

It was at least the tenth time Goodwin heard the recording taken from the small listening device planted yesterday in Adam's car. He listened again as he played it back for Deputy Director Quinn.

"And that's when he slugged the cop?" Quinn asked.

"Wasn't much of a slug, but yeah, that was the assault."

"Any idea where he was headed or who he was referring to?"

"No, he didn't give any indication or mention any names while driving. The whole thing just seemed to happen. One minute he was enjoying a dinner out with his future sister-in-law, the next minute he was a raving lunatic. Knocked over a couple of tables inside the restaurant, flattened the maitre d', and nearly sent an elderly couple to their eternal rest on the way out. If Thomas and I weren't already facing southbound when he jumped into his car, I doubt we would have been able to keep up with him." Goodwin paused to take a drag of his cigarette. "He was arrested at nine o'clock and spent the night in the Barnstable jail. The Allsworth woman arrived about an hour ago and I assume posted bail.

They're headed back to Boston now," Goodwin added, as he maneuvered around a pick-up truck going about fifteen miles below the speed limit.

"Good job, Rick," Quinn said. "I'm sure you've heard by now about the Senator's assassination."

"About an hour ago," Goodwin confirmed. "His wife found him earlier this morning slumped over his desk. Three bullet wounds. Anything else?"

"Coroner placed the time of death just after eight PM last night. Just about the same time you were chasing our boy around the Cape. Same M.O. as Santiago. A 9mm automatic with a silencer. No signs of forced entry. The security system was engaged, but for some reason not tripped. All doors and windows were locked from the inside. Just doesn't seem to make sense," Quinn said with a trace of frustration. "Our Mystery Man called late last night," he continued a moment later. "He confirmed our suspicions about the Senator. He was chin-deep involved with the Organization."

"Did he know before hand about the assassination?" Goodwin asked.

"If he did, he kept it a secret. I expect he'll call at some point today. I'll keep you informed. Get back to me if anything happens with MacGregor."

"End transmission," Goodwin said to the voice-operated car phone.

It had been a long, painful night cramped behind the wheel of his late-model Chevy. As if it wasn't bad enough having to stake out the tiny Barnstable jail cell all night, he had to do it with a perpetual bore like Thomas. For what seemed an eternity, his partner commented on the extraordinary number of alien abductions, Bigfoot sightings, and countless human oddities found in his collection of ridiculous magazines for inquiring minds.

Through it all though, there was something scratching around in the back of Goodwin's thoughts trying to find its way into clear conscious thought. It was something he felt he should have seen or heard or found strange, but just couldn't quite put his finger on it. He'd been over the sequence of events a thousand times, everything from when MacGregor picked up the Allsworth woman to when she picked him up at the jail, and still nothing seemed out of the ordinary. Yet, he knew there was, just as he knew Thomas would find even more mundane bits of yellow journalism to share with him.

Thankfully, Thomas now slept quietly in the passenger seat, his toupee pathetically slanted to the left, his glasses resting on his forehead, and his 9mm semiautomatic, fully-loaded, on his right thigh. Goodwin wondered how fast he would have to hit a pothole to get the gun to discharge. The angle of the barrel would insure a direct hit into the fleshy part of Thomas' thigh and with any luck put him out of commission for a few months. Of course, it was only wishful thinking and not something he would actually do, but without realizing it, the speedometer in the Chevy quickly traveled from fifty-five to almost seventy.

✳✳✳✳✳✳✳✳✳✳✳✳✳✳✳✳✳✳✳✳✳✳✳✳✳✳✳✳✳✳✳✳✳✳✳

Adam turned off the Southeast Expressway onto Morrissey Boulevard with Paige following close behind. They retrieved Adam's car from the impound lot and agreed to wait until arriving back at his townhouse before discussing the bizarre events of the night before. The snowplows and sanders had performed admirably and the commute from Cape Cod to Boston was swift and unobtrusive. Mark Twain's adage about New England weather changing every few minutes appeared as prophetic today as it was then. The cold front that engulfed the city twenty-four hours ago had given way to bright sunshine, blue skies, and moderate temperatures.

A left at the stop light and quick right onto Commonwealth Avenue brought Adam to Lindsey Place. He parked in his designated spot and waited for Paige to arrive. Without saying a word, they walked slowly to the security doors of the building and took the stairs to his second-floor unit.

The seven room, two bedroom, one and a half bath living area seemed much smaller to Adam than he remembered. His short say in the county jail had made him slightly claustrophobic, not to mention humiliated and dejected.

Plopping himself into one of the two overstuffed armchairs in the living room, he forced himself to make eye contact with Paige.

"I guess I owe you an explanation," he began.

"You don't owe me anything, Adam," she said, taking a step toward him. Kneeling beside the chair, she took his hand gently into hers. "I'm worried about you, that's all. If there's something wrong, I want to help. I want to be there for you."

A surge of emotion, like an electrical current, rushed unrestrained through his body. Inside, he burned with desire. Outside, he flushed with embarrassment.

The sudden compulsion to lean over and kiss her was again upon him. Her emerald green eyes and lips as soft and sweet as the finest red wine seemed to grab onto that compulsion and pull him dangerously close to acting upon his desire.

"You're a very special person Paige. If I ever pulled a stunt like this with your sister, I think I would have preferred prison life with a guy named Bubba than having to face her wrath," he said with a faint smile.

"Please, don't compare me to Allison," she said, trying to return his smile. "Why don't you change out of those clothes and I'll make us a fresh pot of coffee. You look like you could use a pot or two."

Twenty minutes later he joined her at the kitchen table, each with a hot mug in front of them. While in the shower, he rehearsed a hundred different times on how to begin his explanation and a hundred different times they sounded perfect. Now as he gazed longingly into her eyes, he felt his tongue begin to swell beyond the size of his mouth. Placing the cup back onto the saucer, Adam took a deep breath and tried to begin. "Paige, the last couple of days I've been…well, I've been experiencing rather abnormal behavior."

"Similar to last night," she asked concerned.

"Exactly like last night," he said. "It actually began a few weeks ago with migraines, nightmares, and the occasional insomnia. But Monday morning something really bizarre happened. Come with me," he said, leading her to his bedroom.

An audible gasp escaped Paige's lips as she saw the utter chaos in Adam's room. Pieces of broken wood were strewn about, clothing covered the floor, and a dresser and nightstand were tipped over onto their sides.

"I'm afraid it gets worse," he said. "After my shower Monday morning, I was standing in front of this mirror trying to decide which tie to wear. The next thing I remember is this," he said, pointing to the words still scrawled across their reflection.

"My God, Adam. Is that blood?" Paige asked.

"My blood. I blacked-out for twenty-eight minutes, during which time, I went to the kitchen, got a knife, came back here and sliced my hand, then wrote those words. We won't even go into what I was wearing."

"He's coming? What does it mean? Who's coming?" she asked totally confused.

"That's just it, I have no idea. Before I picked you up last night, I met with a psychiatrist in Brookline. He thinks I may have suffered a fugue."

"My God, they have a name for this?" she asked surprised.

"Apparently they're not all that uncommon," Adam said calmly, hoping to quell the fear he sensed in her. "They can be symptomatic of many things ranging from a small stroke to Alzheimer's to a simple build-up of stress and anxiety. The doctor seemed to think I fell into the last category."

"C'mon Adam, You're the last person in the world to get stressed about anything. Besides, I doubt anyone could experience this sort of behavior simply from stress. You're not telling me everything. Please, I need to know," she said with a slight tremble in her voice.

This time it was Adam who took her hand gently into his own. "Paige, honest, the doctor didn't seem to think there was any real reason for concern. Not right now anyway. Besides, I had a full physical yester-day and Doctor Jellison gave me a clean bill of health. No heart trouble, no brain tumor, no early signs of Alzheimer's, and no blood clots, noth-ing at all. I'm sure what I've experienced is strictly psychological. And I'm certain once I take care of certain issues, 'cleanse my soul' as the doctor put it; these problems will all dissipate."

As hard as he tried to convince Paige his condition was not serious or permanent, he could see in her eyes he had failed. A small tear had emerged from the corner of her eye and both eyes were slightly red. He could feel her small hand in his shaking and her palms had a nervous wetness to them.

He pulled her gently into his arms and she rested her head on his shoulder. It was worth suffering al the fugues in the world just to hold her in his embrace. He felt slightly lightheaded, almost intoxicated, by her wonderfully scented hair and her warm breath along the back of his neck.

"Have you told Allison, yet?" she asked, causing the spell and embrace to end simultaneously.

Adam gently wiped a tear from Paige's cheek, savoring the intimacy a second longer before turning abruptly.

"What's wrong, Adam? What did I say?" Paige asked, confused by his sudden change in attitude.

"Paige, please don't think poorly of me. I know Allison is your sister, but…but I'm just not sure I'm in love with her or ever have been for that matter," he said turning to face her once again.

The look on Paige's face was so intense Adam was sure she could see right through him, past the walls of the bedroom, and into the street.

"It was my intention to end the relationship with her last night after dinner, but, well you know what happened before I had a chance."

"Adam, I'm sorry," she began slowly, taken back by the announce-ment. "This is such a surprise. I always thought you were happy with Allison. I guess I just assumed you were as enamored with her charms as everyone else seems to be.

"And I don't think poorly of you at all. To tell you the truth, I never thought you and Allison were quite right for each other anyway. As awful as it may sound, I felt you deserved better," she said.

Passion again began to surge from deep within his soul. More than anything he wanted to hold her, hug her, and tell her his real feelings for her.

"Paige, I don't know why or when I stopped having feelings for Allison, but there's no doubt it happened. However," he continued quickly, "my feelings for you in no way compromised my feelings for her."

Adam mustered the courage to look her in the eyes as he spoke and noticed the confusion he saw in her.

"I don't understand Adam. How could the feelings you have for me change the way you feel about Allison?"

Please don't make this anymore difficult than it already is, he thought.

Stepping closer to Paige, he tried to begin again. "Paige…Oh hell, Paige, I love you. I've loved you for quite sometime but was too stupid to realize it."

As if no longer in control of his thoughts or actions, Adam leaned over and softly pressed his lips against her mouth. The seconds seemed like an eternal bliss as he savored the wetness of her tongue and felt the lift of her breasts against his chest. Even more amazing than the courage it took for him to begin the kiss was the fact it continued with no resistance.

He felt her arms circle his neck, pulling him deeper into the embrace. Patiently, his hands slid over the firmness of her buttocks, slowly reaching up under the hem of her dress. He gently traced the back of her thighs with his fingers. Their mouths separated for a moment, as Paige arched her head, giving herself completely to his desire. Kissing her neck along the collarbone, he carefully worked his lips down her throat, the vibration of her groans only exciting him more. Her arms pressed down on his shoulders, his mouth caressing the soft weight of her breasts through the silk blouse.

Evenly, he slid her panties down the length of her burning thighs, as she lifted one leg, then the other. As their separate desires melded into one, Adam lifted her from the floor and placed her gently onto the tipped bureau.

"I've always loved you Adam. Always," she whispered breathlessly, feeling the cold mahogany against her buttocks as Adam lifted her skirt above her waist.

Placing her thighs around his hips, he gently, but firmly, entered her. In that moment, the world around them no longer existed, taking with it all their problems with it. They feverishly began to explore the depths of their passion and discovered a place within that was still untainted. Adrift in a world of prurience, they simultaneously felt a jolt of pleasure, then trembled, stiffened, and went limp in each other's arms.

Omega stood alone in the observation room watching the children as they learned the various disciplines of self-defense. There were nine altogether, all the same age, all bearing a similar likeness to one another. Within seven years, their sperm would be used in the multiplication of the Organization's army.

Two of the children, numbers two and seven, already displayed a limited ability to teleport. Child number four had the remarkable gift of kinesthetics. The other six also displayed unique talents in various fields of human development.

Omega sighed heavily while watching them interact with one another. His shoulders hung forward and his chin rested squarely on his chest. He carried the look of a man who had been beaten badly by life and was praying for the towel to be mercifully thrown in.

It had been a long night with little sleep and even less peace. The Board members were brought together for an emergency session and were updated on Alec's disappearance.

Emotions from shock to fear to outrage permeated the four-hour meeting. In the end, it was decided Omega was to accept full responsibility for the catastrophe and he alone would bear the brunt of the Board's indignation.

They had assigned Doctor Wenzler temporary control of the situation and in the process had ordered Adam MacGregor be made to undergo reprogramming and to be used as bait in the recapture of Alec.

Bait.

His son was to be used as bait.

If necessary, Wenzler wouldn't hesitate to order Adam's death if he could not be taken alive.

That was the fundamental difference between him and Wenzler. Mac loved and cared for each of the Organization's children. They were the future of the Organization, but they were still children. They needed understanding, guidance, and most of all, love.

To Wenzler, the children, Adam and Alec included, were simply experiments. They were created by and for the benefit of science. They were no more human than a chair or table. Their very existence served one and only one purpose; to further the strength of the Organization. If and when they could no longer serve that function, their elimination was as easy to order as a fast-food meal.

How many times had Wenzler lectured him, "Omega, there is no room in this Organization for sentimentality. The things that we, that I, create are not human. They aren't like you and I. We are on the verge of a great success. Alec is the first of his kind. The first of a new race. A race which is perfect in every way, shape, and form and totally subservient to their creators. To us and the Organization. The ones who die during the experimentation stage are not human children and you have to stop thinking of them as such. They were not born into this world for any purpose other than to further our cause. You must always remember that, my friend."

And now the one child he loved most of all, perhaps even more than his own life was to undergo painful reprogramming. If he survived, Adam would have no memory of Mac, their life together, or the love they shared. He would be nothing more than a human puppet for the Organization.

As Omega watched the children practice their newly taught skills, he realized he always knew this time would come. A time when he would have to choose between the Organization and Adam.

Martin West was right. Men have no business tampering with God's creations. He had no right to decide issues of life and death based on his own narrow viewpoints.

The Organization had gone too far. Though the purpose was noble and pure, the means for attaining it had gone wrong.

In that moment, a plan began to form, not only to save Adam, but just as important, to end the Organization.

****

CHAPTER *Twenty*

The scent was unfamiliar, as was the surrounding area and the noise from above. Slowly opening his eyes against the backdrop of daylight, Alec shivered uncontrollably.

He was wet, cold and confused, but he knew he was free.

Free at last!

The recall had failed to pull him back. Somehow he had been able to teleport from the Senator's home and reappear somewhere other than the Institute.

But where? And how long ago?

Was it the next day, a week later; was he still in the same state or even the same country?

The face of the Imposter smiled at him from the deeply engraved memory of the photograph. The evil eyes of the Lookalike were taunting his very existence. The man responsible for stealing his happiness, his parents, his childhood and his life was still alive. Anger and hatred swelled up inside him like a balloon ready to burst.

He was free though, and no matter where he was or how long removed, nothing would stop him now from extracting vengeance. Nothing would stop him from dispensing justice in the name of the Organization.

He lifted himself from the frost-covered lawn and looked about for some indication of his whereabouts. In front of him, a hundred and fifty yards of greenish-brown grass separated him from the back of a large white farmhouse. An old tire swing swung lazily in the cold breeze from a tree limb. Several old cars, all missing a tire or door or engine cluttered most of the yard. A wash line was pulled tightly from the back porch and several pieces of clothing dangled down.

Behind him, the roar of a passing truck and several cars flew past on the highway.

A stream, frozen by the winter air, ran under the overpass.

Cold and hungry, Alec felt for the 9mm pistol tucked in his damp trousers before beginning the slow walk across the lawn toward the house.

Sleeping beauty was the first thing Adam thought of as he stared longingly at Paige, though in no way did he feel like Prince Charming of the fairy tale. For whatever reasons, regardless of the deep felt emotion and sincerity, he had seduced and made love to his fiancée's sister. Not only had he insured his relationship with Allison was now going to be a messy affair, he had dragged Paige into it as well.

Conflicting emotions pulled at him as he continued to watch her sleep. On one hand, he was lying next to the one woman he truly loved. A woman who made him feel complete and worthy, and gave purpose to his existence.

However, on the other hand, feelings of doubt, betrayal, and deception weighed down his euphoria. It was bad enough that his life was messed up, but it was unforgivable that he dragged Paige's life down with him.

In the true essence of the word, he and Paige had made love three times before dozing off in the naked embrace of one another. Adam was sure Noah Webster had yet to find words describing the feelings of satisfaction and joy he felt upon each climatic peak.

Gently sweeping a lock of hair from her forehead, he closed his eyes for a moment to savor the excitement and passion they shared only a couple of hours before. When his lids opened again, he was staring into a pool of liquid green.

"How long have we been asleep?" Paige asked. A smile crept along the edges of her mouth, and her eyes twinkled in a way that suggested she had no misgivings about what transpired between them.

"About two hours," Adam said, returning the smile. "It's almost two o'clock."

Just when he needed it most, when the guilt of his infidelity was getting the best of him, Paige rested her head on his chest and said, "I love you, Adam."

He pulled her closer, but before he could return the words, the phone startled them both.

On the second ring, Adam answered.

"Adam, thank God I've found you," Mac said in a hurried voice. "Your secretary told me that you hadn't between to the office today, and she hadn't heard from you. Are you all right?"

"Mac, I...I'm sorry. I had some personal business to take care of," Adam stammered. "I had to...."

"Never mind that," Mac interrupted, his voice carrying an unfamiliar tone. "Adam, I don't have time to explain everything right now. But for the love of God, please listen carefully and do just as I say."

"Mac, what's going on? Are you in some sort of trouble?"

"Senator Allsworth is dead, Adam. The people responsible are coming after you."

"Dead! Me? Mac, I...."

Before he could continue, three loud knocks echoed in the bedroom.

"'Mac, hold on one second, there's someone at the door," Adam said, as he lifted himself from the bed.

"Don't answer it, Adam! Get out! Get out of the house!"

Even before Mac finished his warning, the sound of splintering wood caused Adam to drop the phone and rush to the living room.

Two men, both armed, stopped him in mid-step.

"Get dressed," one of them said with a grin, the gun pointed at Adam's chest. "You're going for a little ride."

The second one slid passed Adam and into the bedroom. Pointing the gun at Paige, he said, "Should I kill his bitch now or take her with us?"

"Bring her along," the first man said. "We'll let Wenzler decide what to do with her."

"What the hell's going on?" Adam demanded.

His reply was a vicious right hook with the butt of a Glock automatic pistol. He stumbled back and tripped over the ottoman.

"I said to get dressed," the man replied calmly. "I'm getting paid to bring you in dead or alive. The choice is yours."

The man with Paige smiled at her trembling nakedness, and hung up the phone.

****

Chapter *Twenty-One*

The woman appeared at the door wiping her hands on the base of her faded, food-stained apron. A lock or two of stringy gray hair spread beyond the hairnet and matted to her forehead. She looked older than her age would suggest and carried with her the burden of life. Only forty-three years old, Martha Henderson was a single mother of five, her oldest only ten. Her husband had walked out on her two years ago, leaving her to support the family by way of state-funded relief and the occasional task of taking in laundry.

It was in the middle of such a task that the strange young man appeared at her back door.

"I'm sorry to disturb you ma'am," Alec began. "I've run out of gas up on the highway, and I was wondering if you'd mind letting me use the phone?"

Martha gave him the once over, noting his disheveled clothing and unkempt hair, then, because it was her nature to do so, held the door open and offered her assistance.

"Come in," she said. "The phone is on the wall next to the stove."

"Thank you," Alec answered with feigned gratitude.

He quickly scanned the kitchen area, finding it both cluttered and messy. Five or six pans, a handful of dishes, and a few glasses were stacked haphazardly in the basin. The floor had a noticeable layer of dirt, and the walls were marked with fingerprints, grime, and crayon.

However, none of those things fully registered with Alec, because the moment he began scanning the area, his nostrils were treated to the scent of homemade bread and soup.

"I hope it's a local call. I can't afford no more bills," Martha said, closing the door behind her.

Snatched from the heavenly aroma, Alec assured her it was and walked to the phone. Picking up the receiver, he randomly punched seven digits.

While pretending to be talking with a service station, Alec made a mental note of the area code printed to the phone. He recognized it immediately as being a Massachusetts number. *At least I haven't teleported out of the state*, he thought.

"They say they can come in about a half hour. Would you mind if I rested a bit? I've had a long night," Alec said.

Again Martha hesitated. Something about the man seemed strange and awkward.

But she was too trusting, too naïve, too quick to accept people as honest and trustworthy. At least that's what Frank, her missing husband, had said the morning he left.

Against her better judgment, she offered him a seat in the kitchen, removing a bundle of dirty laundry from the chair.

"I don't have much, but if you like, I can spare a bowl of soup and a couple slices of bread," she offered.

"You're very kind. If your husband wouldn't object, I'd love some."

"If that son of a bitch ever returns, I'll be sure to ask him. But right now, it's just me and the boys, and we don't mind none."

"Boys," Alec asked, still trying to size up the situation.

"My sons. Five of them actually. Quite a handful. They're out front playing."

Alec thought of his own mother. *Why wasn't she capable of loving more than one son? What had the Imposter told her that she would willingly abandon her oldest child?*

A sudden longing washed over him like an unexpected summer shower. He wanted to be loved and cared for. He wanted a mother like Martha. A mother who would stand by him no matter what difficulty fate dealt her. No matter how many brothers, how little money, or how much pain life caused.

"Do all your boys look like their donor?" Alec asked solemnly.

"Donor?" Martha repeated. "That's a strange way to put it. If you mean their father, then yes, they all resemble Frank. He was quite a looker," Martha said angling the ladle into an empty bowl.

"My brother looks exactly like me. Same hair, same eyes, same face. Everything," Alec said with a tinge of rage behind the words.

"How nice. You're a twin," she said innocently.

"He may look like me, but we're not the same. He may have been able to fool my mother and the Organization, but he can't fool me. He's evil, and he has to be destroyed. I have to kill him to protect Omega and the others," Alec said, suddenly on his feet. "You can help me Martha. You can help kill this demon before he ruins everything. While there's still time. Will you help me?" The rage in Alec's eyes and the conviction in his voice caused Martha to drop the bowl of soup and bring her hands to her mouth. Her heart racing wildly, her thoughts stifled by fear she tried to scream, but could only manage a short gasp.

"No," Alec pleaded, "don't be afraid of me. That's what he wants. He wants you to think I'm the bad one, that I'm the one who needs to be destroyed. You believe me, don't you Martha? You believe that the Imposter must be stopped," Alec said, shaking the terrified woman by the shoulders.

With strength derived only from primal fear, she pushed Alec away. The sudden and unexpected thrust caught him by surprise, and he stumbled backward, tripping over a chair. Quickly scrambling to his feet, he reached behind him and removed the semi-automatic from his waistband.

"He's gotten to you too, hasn't he? You're on his side. You're as evil as he is, and evil must be destroyed."

The frightened woman tried to run from the room, but Alec caught her by the hair and pulled her down to the floor. A second later, with her windpipe crushed, and her eyes bulging from their sockets, Martha Henderson laid dead on her kitchen floor.

With short, heavy breaths, Alec got to his feet and walked toward the stove. Picking up the bowl and ladle from the floor, he poured himself a generous helping of soup, and sat back at the kitchen table.

He would eat first, then deal with the evil woman's offspring.

****

Adam and Paige were forced from the townhouse, down the stairs, and onto the walkway leading to the parking lot. To Adam, none of it made sense. Not the fugues or the images they conjured, not the kidnapping, and especially not Mac's admonition on the telephone.

"The Senator's dead. The people responsible are coming for you. Get out of the house."

What the hell did it all mean? What possible motive could the Senator's murder have with him? What sublime connection was there to all that was happening?

"The black limo," the man behind Adam said. "You get in first. You try any of that disappearing shit or anything that remotely appears to be an escape attempt and your girlfriend here gets the first bullet. Is that understood?"

Adam nodded, keeping his eyes directed ahead.

Just as he reached the car and was about to open the rear door, a loud snap, like the rush of air, was immediately followed by the painful groan from the man behind him.

There were two more snaps of air from a cluster of trees in front of him and to the left.

Gunshots? Silencers?

Paige's captor immediately threw her to the ground.

Ignoring her for the moment, he took refuge behind the limo, and began firing wildly into the dense trees. With his head down, Adam grabbed Paige's arm and forced her to her feet.

"Move, Move!" he yelled over the thundering exchange of gunfire, pushing her toward several of the parked cars.

Crouching behind a yellow Subaru, they watched in shock, as a scene from an old western shootout played before them. Adam's captor was still motionless, a puddle of redness growing rapidly around him.

"Are you all right?' Adam asked, as they lay behind the car.

"I think so!" she said breathlessly. "What's happening Adam? What's going on?"

Adam couldn't answer her because one, he was surveying the parking lot for a possible means of escape, and two, he had no idea what was going on.

Three cars behind them and across the lot, he saw Paige's Grand Am. She also caught his glance.

"Give me your keys," he said without looking at her.

"Adam, no, it's suicide. We'd have to cross at least twenty yards of open space. It'll be like shooting ducks in a barrel."

"Our only other option," Adam said harsher than he intended, "is to wait it out and see who wins at the OK Corral. But we have no assurances the gunmen in the woods are good guys. It's the only way Paige. Get ready."

✶✶✶✶✶✶✶✶✶✶✶✶✶✶✶✶✶✶✶✶✶✶✶✶✶✶✶✶✶✶✶✶✶

Goodwin was alone in the parking lot of Adam's townhouse when the black limo pulled into the complex. Quinn had sent Thomas to a medical building in Cambridge to check out a possible lead on the identity of Omega.

He watched intently, as the two men removed themselves from the vehicle and made their way to the steps of Adam's building. They were dressed in fashionable two-piece suits, and the jacket of one showed a considerable bulge just above the belt line. Goodwin knew it was a handgun of some sort.

He radioed ahead for back up, then took up a strategic position in the dense woods, fifteen yards in front of the limo. After twenty minutes, he began to feel silly and thought he had overreacted. Just as he started back to his car though, he saw the four of them leaving the townhouse.

Adam, a woman he knew to be Paige Allsworth, and the two men from the limo, walked stiffly toward the parking lot. The men were scanning the area, keeping a tight rein on their prisoners. Goodwin was afraid he wouldn't be allowed a clear shot, but just as they reached the car, Adam's captor said something and pushed him toward the back passenger door.

Goodwin squeezed the trigger gently and a millisecond later watched, as one of the men feel to the ground. The bullet found its mark just below the man's chin. The second man realized what happened and pushed the Allsworth woman to the ground, as he scurried behind the limo. Goodwin saw Adam grab the girl and quickly take refuge behind one of the other vehicles.

He knew the second man couldn't see him, but damn if his bullets were coming awfully close. He fired several more shots into the limo, hoping to keep the man in check until backup arrived. Reloading his automatic, he saw Adam and Paige dart from the yellow Subaru and begin sprinting toward another car across the lot.

He stood and emptied his freshly loaded revolver into the limo, trying to offer as much cover as possible. It worked. Both Paige and Adam were inside the car. The faint, but growing sound of sirens could be heard a mile or so away. In a few minutes, backup would arrive and the man would either be forced to surrender or be killed.

★★*★*★*★*★*★*★*★*★*★*★*★*★*★*★*★*★*★*

The Grand Am started on the first attempt, and Adam threw it into reverse. He couldn't use the driveway that led onto Commonwealth Avenue, because it would mean driving between the two gunmen. Instead, he threw the car into gear and raced the engine, as the car jumped the foot-high concrete barrier. The impact caught Paige by surprise, and her head hit hard against the dashboard. A slow trickle of blood quickly covered the left side of her face.

The car held fast to the slick grass, as Adam pushed the pedal to the floor. The inclined landscaping led to the sidewalk in front of Adam's townhouse, and the tires peeled, as they gripped the asphalt. They were now directly in back of the gunman who forced his way into Adam's apartment.

Suddenly, the back window blew apart, as pieces of the gummy windshield flew into the front seat and showered them with odd-shaped chards of glass. Thirty yards in front of them was the wire fence separating the complex from the street.

More shots and the front windshield cracked into a spider web design, as two bullets screeched in through the busted-out back window. The windshield remained intact though, showing two small holes that whistled with the passing wind.

Fifteen yards to the fence.

Ten yards.

Five yards.

Two police cars, sirens blaring, sped past seconds before Adam crashed the gate and swung hard onto Commonwealth Avenue. Crumpled and bent fencing hung to his front bumper, as his car clipped a pick-up truck, and spun out of control.

In front of them, on-rushing traffic swerved and skidded. The eerie sound of metal scraping metal echoed the neighborhood.

Adam slammed the Grand Am into reverse, changed direction, and raced between two other visibly dented cars.

Three minutes later, as the bullet riddled Grand Am entered onto the expressway, Adam turned to Paige. One side of her face was pale white, the other, bright red.

"Were you hit," he asked quickly, maneuvering into the breakdown lane.

"No! Don't stop," Paige pleaded in a voice discerning with fear. "Please, don't stop!"

"You have to drive," Adam said calmly. "I've been shot."

****

Omega gave each of the children a long hug and told each one how much he loved them. "Better things are waiting for each of you on the other side," he told the group of nine. "Better things."

The children thought nothing of the comment as they happily ate the ice cream Omega brought them. A couple of times each week, Omega made it a point to bring the children a surprise. His reward was the smiles on their faces and the grateful hugs they were always eager to share. This morning though, Omega would not be rewarded. This morning would be the children's last surprise and their last chance to smile.

Before his phone call to Adam, he called the local branch of the FBI and gave directions to Special Agent Thomas to meet him at the Keisler Institute for Genetic Research. It was time to expose the Organization and with any luck save Adam.

The ice cream he brought the children was laced with heavy doses of cyanide, which, at the very least, would render them unconscious. He knew though, not all of them would die. Their advanced immune systems would fight the effects of the poison while they slept. It was because of that; Omega planted plastic explosives throughout the facility. They were timed to explode within thirty minutes.

Plenty of time to give Agent Thomas all the information and documented evidence he would require for indictments against the Organization. He gave the children one last hug and kiss, told them again how much he loved them, and then left them with the remainder of the ice cream.

✳✳✳✳✳✳✳✳✳✳✳✳✳✳✳✳✳✳✳✳✳✳✳✳✳✳✳✳✳✳✳✳✳✳✳

Alec placed the five dead boys next to their dead mother and shook his head angrily.

"How many others have you infected with your evil, brother? How many more am I going to have to kill before I get to you?" he asked.

He knew of at least one more person he would have to kill before he could discover Adam's whereabouts. The woman in the photo, the one with her arms around the Impostor. Before killing her though, he would make her tell him where the coward was hiding. He had been subjected to every type of torture known to the Organization, and the thought of carrying out a few of the more horrendous ones on the woman excited him terribly.

The only concern was how to get to her. He knew he could teleport back to the Senator's house, but assumed it was probably crawling with FBI and local police. Time was on his side though. There was no recall. No sense of urgency. No one to give him a time line. This was his mission, and it would be up to him to decide when and where to strike next.

Yes, the woman would tell him where the Lookalike was, and then the fun could begin. The years of suffering in a vast blackness would be put to rest. He could return to the facility a hero, admired by his handlers, praised by Omega, and gratefully received by Wenzler.

Satisfied with his course of action, Alec stepped over the dead bodies on the kitchen floor and helped himself to another bowl of soup.

✳✳✳✳✳✳✳✳✳✳✳✳✳✳✳✳✳✳✳✳✳✳✳✳✳✳✳✳✳✳✳✳✳✳✳

When the man behind the limo stood to fire at the fleeting Grand Am, Goodwin took careful aim and fired two quick shots in succession. Both bullets slammed into the man's back and sent him to the asphalt face first.

Goodwin watched as the Grand Am crashed the wire fence and bolted onto the street. Racing back to his own car in hopes of pursuing Adam, he instead found himself facing four armed policemen.

"Police! Move away from the car and drop your weapon," a young officer yelled from behind his open door.

"FBI," Goodwin yelled back. "I'm in hot pursuit of a late model Grand Am."

"Drop the gun now," the officer yelled again.

Realizing the futility of arguing with local police, Goodwin lowered his gun and let it fall to the ground. Two officers quickly approached him, handcuffed his hands behind his back, and roughly frisked him.

"I'm FBI. My ID is inside my wallet," Goodwin said angrily. It was one thing to be detained, another to be treated like public enemy number one.

The young officer who initially told him to drop his weapon chuckled and said, "Yeah and I'm J. Edgar Hoover, asshole."

The car radio in Goodwin's car suddenly came to life.

"Rick," the voice said urgently. "Rick, are you there?"

The young officer smiled and reached into the car. "Looks like your partner's checking up on you," he said smugly.

Picking up the receiver, the officer said, "Your boy's not taking any calls right now asshole."

"Who the hell is this?" the voice said angrily.

"Officer Mark Lebbossiere of the Boston Police Department. I don't suppose you want to tell me who you are?" he said confidently, enjoying the game.

'This is Deputy Director Quinn of the Federal Bureau of Investigation. I hope to God you have other career options, Office Lebbossiere."

The officer went pale and mumbled incoherently to himself.

****

CHAPTER *Twenty-Two*

Wenzler threw open the door to Omega's office and glared menacingly through his gray eyes. "The children. What have you done to the children?"

The loud intrusion startled Omega for a moment, then he rose calmly from behind his desk. "I've taken the necessary precautions, Doctor," he said deliberately. "I've made sure that neither you nor the Organization could use them any longer."

Holding his hand out, he gestured to the man in the corner of the office. "This is Special Agent Thomas of the FBI. I'm sure you two will be spending a great deal of time together in the near future."

Thomas pulled his gun when the door had swung open. He stood in a shooters crouch and stared quietly at the doctor.

"What has he told you?" the Doctor asked, still in a very angry tone.

"Enough to send you and your cronies to prison for a very long time, Doctor. A very long time."

"I've never trusted you Omega, but I never thought you'd be the one to sell us out. Why? Why now?"

Omega walked around his desk and stood in front of Wenzler. "Martin was right all those years ago, Doctor. We have no right playing judge and jury with societies' ills. And more importantly, we have no right creating life for the sole purposes of the Organization. The day Martin died, he told me people who become obsessed with destroying evil, can't help but become evil themselves. I understand now what he meant."

"Always the sentimental one Omega. Were we evil when we killed the man who raped and murdered your wife? Were we evil when we dispensed justice to the countless number of felons who escaped our legal system? Were we evil when we allowed you to adopt Adam? I'm curious Omega, at what point did we become evil? Was it when the Organization could no longer serve your selfish interests?"

The three of them were quiet for a moment, and then Wenzler turned to Thomas. "Two of the children are dead. The other seven are unconscious, but they'll live. Lose those files. Tell your boss it was a hoax and get back to Adam. I have no doubt Alec will be able to find him soon."

"What about him?" Thomas said, nodding in the direction of Omega.

"Kill him and dump his body far from here. I'll be joining a field team in Worcester. Six dead bodies were reported, five boys and a mother. We have reason to believe it was Alec."

Omega stared in disbelief at the conversation. Thomas was one of them. Wenzler had his own private army of recruits. His shoulders slumped, and his jaw slackened at the realization he would not be able to save Adam after all. Worst still, Wenzler wouldn't be in the facility when it exploded.

"You heard the man," Thomas said tauntingly to Omega. "And try not to worry about your boy. I'm sure he'll be joining you in hell very shortly," he finished, as he leveled a single bullet into the forehead of a still-stunned Mac MacGregor.

✳✳✳✳✳✳✳✳✳✳✳✳✳✳✳✳✳✳✳✳✳✳✳✳✳✳✳✳✳✳✳✳✳

The bullet entered just below Adam's right shoulder and blood poured freely from the wound. Already he was starting to feel weak and disorientated. Paige tried as gingerly as haste would allow to help him into the passenger seat. When he was finally situated, she hurried back to the driver's side to continue their flight to God knew where. The back of the seat was soaked with wet, sticky blood as she pressed herself into the car.

"No doctors, Paige," Adam said, barely above a whisper. "By law, they have to report any gunshot wound to the authorities. Too easy to trace," he finished with difficulty.

"But Adam, you've been shot. You need medical attention," she said, her voice filled with fear and panic.

But he didn't answer. With the Grand Am approaching seventy-five miles per hour, she glanced quickly at Adam's closed eyes and labored breathing.

Fifteen minutes later, she pulled up to the employee entrance of the Pine Street Inn and raced inside for help. Jim Black, a longtime custodian and a one-time resident of the Inn, helped Paige remove Adam from the car and carry him to a vacant second floor bedroom.

"Nobody must know he's here Jim. Do you understand? I need to know I can trust you," she pleaded.

"They won't hear it from me Ms. Allsworth, but you can't just leave him here. He'll die."

Paige looked at Adam's motionless body and shivered.

He'll die, she thought.

"Jim, I need you to run to Doctor Richards' office and tell him I have an emergency. Tell him one of our residents was shot, but don't give him any details. Just tell him to come right away," Paige said, pushing the man through the door as she spoke. "Hurry Jim, please."

Paige moved quickly to the bathroom and pulled out an old porcelain basin. Filling it with hot water, she retrieved several washcloths. Hurrying back to Adam's side, she carefully dipped the cloth into the water and gently caressed the wound.

Amazingly, the bleeding had stopped and as she washed away the dried blood, she could see the hole in his back from the bullet. She dipped the cloth again, and continued to clean the hole as best she could.

On her third attempt to clean the wound, she gasped as she stared in amazement at the small cylinder shaped abyss. The hole was still blackish-red, but something was happening. She saw it, but what she saw was too strange and incomprehensible to register completely. She held the washcloth to her chest, as the bullet in Adam's back continued to push its way from the hole.

It fell unceremoniously to the floor and laid still next to her foot. She froze at the sight of it; afraid the slightest movement might bring it back to life. Seconds passed into minutes before she finally looked away from the bullet and back toward Adam. The hole was gone. There was no scar, no bruising, and no redness. Nothing to indicate the wound of a few minutes ago.

Adam groaned softly and rolled onto his freshly healed back.

The white two-story farmhouse was in a rural district of Worcester. Its nearest neighbor was some five hundred yards away, through thick trees and an unpaved back road.

Wenzler arrived on the scene by way of helicopter, along with two members of his selected field team. The Worcester Chief of Police was a sympathetic member of the rapidly decaying Organization and so it was no problem keeping the locals from tampering with or unwittingly stumbling upon evidence of Alec's handiwork.

With his head low, Wenzler exited the helicopter and walked briskly toward the crime scene. A half-dozen uniformed police officers and several plain-clothes detectives' from the Worcester Police Station stood about idly. They gave Wenzler and his two companions a contemptuous stare before stepping aside, allowing the three of them under the yellow tape surrounding the area.

Chief Samuel Wilson was the first to greet them as they came upon the back stairs.

"Christ Doctor, it's about time. My men are pretty upset and are starting to ask questions about why I'm delaying their investigation. They want to know why outsiders are being allowed onto the scene before themselves," the Chief said.

It was without a doubt the first time Wilson had ever spoken to Wenzler without his usual syrupy tone.

"I don't give a shit about you or your country bumpkin cops. Keep them at bay until I tell you otherwise. Is that clear?" Wenzler said as he passed by the Chief without waiting for a response. "What do we know so far?" he asked loudly upon entering the kitchen.

One of the forensic specialists hurried over to where Wenzler was standing.

"No doubt about it sir. It was our boy. We've got his fingerprints everywhere. The woman had her throat crushed and each of the five boys was shot once in the back of the head. All were killed with a 9mm semi-automatic, same as Alec was carrying when he disappeared from Allsworth's house."

"How long have they been dead?"

"No more than two hours. Only slight signs of rigor mortis and the body temperature is still above seventy degrees."

Wenzler was silent for a moment as he eyed the kitchen area, then the small hallway leading to the living room.

"Any witnesses?" he finally asked.

"We don't think so. Nothing concrete anyway. A neighbor up the road thinks she may have seen Alec walking across the yard earlier. The description she gave was pretty genetic though. Probably fit about ninety percent of the white population."

"Kill her," Wenzler said calmly, as if he'd just asked for a glass of water. "Have Johnson and Gates stage an accident of some sort, either tonight or tomorrow morning. I don't want any loose ends."

"I understand sir. Shall I allow the locals in or do you want to keep them waiting?"

"No, let them blunder through their investigation. We're done here. Meet me out front as soon as you give Chief Wilson the go ahead."

Wenzler motioned for the two men from the helicopter to follow him outside and waited until the rest of the team arrived before speaking.

"It's a safe bet this is where Alec teleported to last night. We have confirmed he's been here and in all likelihood is responsible for this massacre. He hasn't teleported without my assistance in many months and may not trust himself to try it alone. Not yet anyway. I want a tap on the DMV records and local police files to determine if there have been any stolen vehicles reported in the last twelve hours. If so, find them and find them fast. I believe our best hopes of recapturing Alec still lie with his brother but that doesn't mean I don't want every possibility, every lead, and every opportunity explored.

"For those of you who haven't heard, Omega is dead. He attempted to betray the Organization and all the good it represents. The only…"

"Doctor! Doctor!" the pilot shouted over the roar of the helicopter. "You have a priority one message sir."

"Wait here," he instructed the cluster of men and hurried to the helicopter. "Wenzler here," he said loudly into the radio.

A minute later, his face ashen, he walked slowly back to his men.

"The facility has been destroyed," he said angrily. "Omega was responsible. The children, all nine of them, are dead. Now gentlemen, more than ever, we must recapture Alec and his brother. Their sperm and DNA are the only links to our former greatness."

✱✱✱✱✱✱✱✱✱✱✱✱✱✱✱✱✱✱✱✱✱✱✱✱✱✱✱✱✱✱✱✱✱✱✱✱

CHAPTER *Twenty-Three*

Alec slowed the stolen Firebird and parked next to the curb about a block from the Allsworth mansion. He walked quickly, like a man with a purpose, like a man with two decades of excess baggage waiting to be unloaded.

From across the street, mixed into a crowd of fifty or so spectators and reporters, Alec watched the goings-on at the mansion. Police cars came and went through the security gates, as FBI agents walked the grounds in search of clues. From where he stood, Alec watched friends and family members hug and cry as they tried consoling one another.

Within the hour, the woman in the photograph finally exited the mansion with two men and entered the backseat of a black sedan. Breaking into a sprint, Alec ran back to the Firebird.

Minutes later he caught up to the sedan and from a safe distance began to follow it. The sedan entered the highway onto Route 3 and drove the speed limit toward Boston. Traffic was light, but Alec figured more and more vehicles would become the norm the closer they got to the city. With an empty highway, both in front of him and behind, Alec maneuvered the Firebird alongside the driver's side of the Sedan and pulled sharply to the right.

Not expecting the impact, the sedan swerved out of control, hitting the guardrail, then careening back toward the Firebird. Alec gently applied his brakes and watched as the spinning ton of metal passed in front of him. Gracefully, almost in slow motion, the sedan slid sideways onto the shoulder and tipped over the declining embankment before coming to a thunderous halt upside-down.

Alec rushed to the wreckage, arriving just as one of the men began crying out for help. The front windshield was smashed, and Alec could easily peer into the vehicle. All three wore safety belts and as a result found themselves suspended in mid-air. The driver was pinned between the seat and the steering wheel. His face was bloody, and Alec doubted he was alive. The other man was even more bloodied and in obvious pain. His legs crossed one another at odd angles, and it was obvious they were both broken.

"Help us," the man pleaded weakly.

Alec tilted his head and upper body as a way of mocking the man's position.

In the back, he heard the woman's soft groans of pain and immediately went to her door. Remarkably, it opened with little resistance, and after unbuckling her seat belt, slid her out of the car. Dragging her by the arms until he reached the Firebird, he roughly pushed her inside. Popping the trunk of his stolen car he removed the tire iron. Working quickly and with a firm quick, he punctured the gas tank of the sedan and watched as gas poured out, surrounding the car and the immediate area.

The man was still crying out in pain, pleading for assistance. The gas fumes were noxious and strong, and within minutes the man's cries were more from fear than pain.

Removing a lighter from his own car, Alec peered once more into the shattered windshield.

"Please," the man begged. "I have a wife and two children. Don't do this. Please, for their sakes, don't do this."

Alec smiled, and his thumb pulled on the flint of the lighter. A flame immediately appeared.

"Dear Jesus, please," the man implored.

Alec stepped back about three feet and placed the flame to the ground. Immediately it came to life with a hunger all it's own, and quickly consumed the gasoline encircling the damaged car. He waited a moment longer, savoring the screams of human agony brought upon by burning flesh.

✳✳✳✳✳✳✳✳✳✳✳✳✳✳✳✳✳✳✳✳✳✳✳✳✳✳✳✳✳✳✳✳✳✳✳✳

His eyes twitched once, then again, before Adam finally had the strength to open them completely. The room was dark with the exception of a small reading lamp in the far corner. The curtains were pulled, but he could see the fading orange daylight reflected against them. There was a chair beside his bed, and his eyes could make out the slight tracings of his clothing draped over the back.

A moment later, the silhouette of a person standing behind the chair came into focus.

"How do you feel?" Paige asked.

Adam took a moment to ponder the question, and then his eyes went wide. "I was shot," he said more as a question than an answer.

"In the back," Paige said, as she flipped the light switch. "Just below your right shoulder. Here's the proof," she said, sitting down next to him.

"The bullet?" he asked, as Paige dropped it in his hand.

"It fell out." "What do you mean, it fell out. Bullets don't just fall out. They need to be removed."

"Not this one Adam. It fell out. I watched it. And then I watched the hole it fell from just seal itself closed. Dr. Richards thought I was crazy. He thoroughly examined the area and found nothing. He thought maybe I was hysterical and just imagined the whole thing."

"I don't understand Paige," Adam said hesitantly. *Had she been hysterical?* He lifted his right arm slowly, bracing for the inevitable pain, but felt none.

"I don't understand either, Adam," she said emotionally, her voice starting to crack. "I don't understand your fugues or why someone would try to kidnap us, while still others lie in ambush. I don't understand the pictures in the shoebox or the mysterious one-armed man!"

Adam sat up straight with the mention of the one-armed man. "You've seen him, Paige? You've seen the one-armed man? Tell me what he looked like, what was his name?"

She sobbed uncontrollably. The fear and anxiety of the past-twenty-four hours finally were defeating her resolve. "I don't know Adam. Just some sick, desperate man. Jones, I think. Peter Jones."

Adam sat on the edge of the bed holding her hands. "Paige, after I was arrested, I asked the desk sergeant who posted my bail. He told me the person didn't want to leave his name, but said he was a friend, and the sergeant told me he was missing his left arm. And before that, at lunch the other day, a one-armed man introduced himself to me as Peter Jones. He said I went to school with his son."

Paige shook her head violently, as if by doing so she could make everything go away. "Adam, what's going on? Who are these people?"
"You mentioned a shoebox with pictures. What did you mean?"

Regaining some of her composure, she said, "The day after I met Peter Jones, a shoebox wrapped in brown paper was waiting for me at the front desk. There was no return address or note, just some very old pictures and a map. And a picture of you and I at that concert on the Common last year."

"Where is it Paige?" Adam said animatedly. "I have to see it."

She nodded and pulled out a drawer in the nightstand next to the bed. Handing the box to Adam, she wiped her face of the streaking tears.

Adam slowly studied each picture with a sense of awe and shock. Like a crooked politician who's been caught on film, he stared in disbelief.

"Do they mean anything to you, Adam?" Paige asked, noting the bewildered expression on his face.

"This farmhouse is exactly like the one in my nightmares. Exactly! And without a doubt, this boy…or that one," he said pointing to the twins, "is me."

"You have a twin?" she asked.

Slowly remembering bits and pieces, he looked into her eyes and said, "I'm not sure."

"You're not sure? How can you forget about a twin brother?" she asked skeptically.

"You can't, unless you were made to forget."

✱✱✱✱✱✱✱✱✱✱✱✱✱✱✱✱✱✱✱✱✱✱✱✱✱✱✱✱✱✱✱✱✱✱✱✱

Allison opened her eyes for the third time but saw nothing. She was blindfolded; her legs tied tightly together, then to the base of a tree. The throbbing pain in her hand quickly reminded her of the nightmare she was living. Her thumb and forefinger on her left hand had been broken. No, not broken, but snapped like a stick.

Alec stood over her with a malicious grin and said, "If you keep passing out every time I break a bone, we could be here for quite sometime. You really should develop a stronger threshold for pain."

"Please, whoever you are, my family is quite rich. They'll pay whatever you ask. Just don't hurt me," she begged, her voice not even attempting to disguise her fear.

"I don't want money, just information. I'll ask you again, and if you don't give me the correct answer this time, I'm going to break your wrist. Where is Adam?"

"Oh God," she cried. "I don't know. I haven't seen him in two days. Honest! Please don't hurt me."

Alec studied her for a moment, then knelt next to Allison. Picking up her left wrist with a firm grasp, he said, "You know Allison, I think you're telling me the truth. So I'll make you a deal. Tell me where you think Adam might be and whom he might be with, and I'll let you go. Fair enough," he said, tightening his grip around her wrist.

Allison would have sold her soul if it meant getting away from her tormentor. Without a second thought, she quickly said, "Paige, my sister. Adam and her spend a great deal of time together. He's probably with her."

"Good, you see we can work together. Now, where can I find this bitch you call a sister?"

Not at all offended by his choice of words, she told him. "Paige spends most of her time at that godforsaken homeless shelter. It's in Boston on Pine Street, but I don't know how to get there. Now please, let me go."

Alec removed a large carving knife he had taken from Martha's kitchen and cut the rope which bound Allison to the tree.

"A deal is a deal," he said, lifting Allison from the ground. "But I can't let you see me or untie your legs until I've had time to get far away. So I'm going to leave you on the side of the road where someone will surely stop to help you," he said, as he carried her further into the woods. "Now you must promise not to remove your blindfold until I've left."

"Anything. Anything you say," she eagerly agreed.

Coming to a halt, he said, "OK, this is where I'm going to leave you."

"Thank you," Alison said, truly grateful for her chance to live.

"Don't mention it." Alec smiled, as he dropped her into the seventy five-foot ravine. He watched her body slam into the side of the cliff, bounce away, then hit the ground below with a sickening thud. He continued to smile and thought, *a sister, how nice.* Then he began to focus on teleporting to the homeless shelter on Pine Street.

"My father's dead, Adam," Paige said without sadness or remorse in her voice.

They had been sitting quietly for ten minutes, Adam studying the pictures, Paige just staring off into space.

"I know," he said, taking her hand in his. "Mac told me just before those men broke into my house. I'm so sorry Paige."

"It's funny Adam," she began in the same flat toned voice, "my father and I were never particularly close. The only time we really spoke was during arguments. I loved him of course, but in a different way than most daughters love their fathers. Now that he's dead, I feel ashamed I'm not more devastated by the news. I don't feel anything at all."

She was silent for a moment, reflecting on her relationship with her father. Adam sat next to her, feeling helpless and at a loss for words to comfort her.

"He knew he was going to be killed, Adam. He knew, and he sent me this," she said, producing the Senator's memo concerning the Organization. "He waited until death before trying to bridge the gap between us. Just like my father."

Adam took the document, but his eyes never left Paige. He had never seen her so distraught or sullen. The hollowness of her voice and the glassy lost look of her stare showed how fragile she was at that very moment. He wanted to reach out to her, tell her everything was going to be all right. But he sensed she needed to deal with the tragedy in her own way, alone and in private.

Reluctantly, his eyes left her and focused on the eight-page document she handed him. He read the Senator's memo through the first time in disbelief. The second time through, he read it in fear. According to the Senator, there existed a vigilante Organization whose members included, amongst others, the Director of the FBI, several hundred federal agents, eight city police chiefs in Massachusetts alone, six senators, and a countless number of highly successful businessmen, doctors, lawyers, and judges. He read about the Organization's function and their scientific breakthroughs in human genetics. And he read about Alec and his amazing powers, and of the children created from his genetically perfected DNA.

Finally, he looked up at Paige. She still seemed distant and aloof, but Adam needed answers. "Paige, your father was a member of this Organization?"

"Apparently," she said with little emotion, still lost in her own little world. "I imagine he was killed because of the document you're holding. I also imagine that the men who tried to kidnap us earlier are also part of the Organization. Either because of what you've been made to forget or because this Organization is afraid of what you'll remember, they want us dead too."

"The farmhouse," Adam said softly. "Paige, we have to go to the farmhouse. I think our answers and my memory can be found there." Almost as an afterthought, he added, "I think I know who Omega is and who Mr. Jones might be."

✳✳✳✳✳✳✳✳✳✳✳✳✳✳✳✳✳✳✳✳✳✳✳✳✳✳✳✳✳✳✳✳✳✳

CHAPTER *Twenty-Four*

It was the first time in months Alec teleported without the help of Dr. Wenzler, and he wasn't disappointed with the results. After stopping briefly at a gas station for a local map, he studied the whereabouts of Pine Street on the city's grid, and when he was sure he knew its location, closed his eyes and focused on his destination. When his head cleared, he found himself standing alone in a trash-strewn alley across the street from The Pine Street Inn.

An unexpected sense of anticipation coursed through his body, and he knew he was close to the Lookalike. Soon his mission would be accomplished and he could return home a hero.

A deeply loved and appreciated hero.

Discretely scanning the area, he crossed the street and walked quickly past the main entrance of the building. Behind the building, he saw the Grand Am with its busted out windows, and suddenly, he knew the evil Imposter was close by. A surge of excitement and pride swelled inside, as he sensed his destiny.

He had killed numerous enemies of the Organization, all in the name of justice and righteousness, but they paled in comparison to the glory and honor that was soon to be his.

He ran a finger alongside the Grand Am as he passed it, feeling the demonic energy course through his veins. Just beyond it, he found the employee's entrance to the building and pulled on the door expecting to find it locked. To his surprise, the door swung open quite easily. Obviously, evil was no match for goodness.

Gray concrete stairwells were to his left, and a freight elevator was to his right. He took the stairs two at a time and quickly arrived at the second floor landing. He didn't know why, but he sensed the Lookalike and his companion were somewhere on the second floor. He could almost feel their evil in the air, taste it in his mouth.

He wiped away a line of sweat just over his brow, then pressed his wet palms against his shirt. Throughout the years, he had found himself in life or death situations and had literally entered fortresses and mansions so heavily guarded, a small army was needed just to get past the front door. But never was he nervous or the least bit afraid. This was different though. This time he was up against evil so black, so perverted, it had swept away his parents and left him wallowing for years in a dark empty abyss of emotional pain.

He gently pulled back the emergency door and peered into the poorly carpeted hallway. It was at that very instant he caught a glimpse of the Impostor and his accomplice just as the doors to the freight elevator closed.

✳✳✳✳✳✳✳✳✳✳✳✳✳✳✳✳✳✳✳✳✳✳✳✳✳✳✳✳✳✳✳✳✳✳✳✳

It was just after four-thirty when Adam and Paige left the second floor bedroom in which he had been resting. Their plan was to drive the beaten Grand Am to the Greyhound Bus Station and once there, rent a car for the trip to upstate New York.

While Adam put together the few items the Inn had available; Paige listened patiently to his theory. He reasoned the child named Alec in the Senator's memo was, in fact, his twin. The same boy who appeared in the old photographs was the same one haunting his nightmares.

"Maybe as children, Alec and I were part of some bizarre scientific experiment. When only Alec showed signs of advanced genetics, they cut me loose. They hypnotized or brainwashed me to forget everything they did to me, to us. But as the bullet wound, or lack of a bullet wound, demonstrates, I do possess some very advanced genes of my own. The block they placed on my memory is beginning to break, and somehow they know this."

He told her about Dr. Leppo's explanation that fugues could be brought on by suppressed memories trying to escape before the conscious mind was ready to deal with them. When he finished, he turned to look at Paige and found her staring at him, but not seeing him. She was somewhere else, buried in her own deeply confused thoughts.

I'm losing her, he thought.

He carried the shoebox under his right arm and grabbed the overnight bag with his left. As they left the room, Paige slid her hand under Adam's elbow as if to say, *I need you.*

He wanted to ask more questions about his amazing recovery and try to delve into the Senator's double life. Just as strongly, he wanted to wrap her up in his embrace and tell her how much he loved her and how he would always be there for her. But he did neither, as they walked quietly and quickly to the freight elevator at the end of the hall. As the doors closed, Adam pushed the ground floor button and accepted Paige's weight, as she leaned gently into him.

✳✳✳✳✳✳✳✳✳✳✳✳✳✳✳✳✳✳✳✳✳✳✳✳✳✳✳✳✳✳✳✳✳✳✳✳

A minute later, when the elevator doors separated on the ground floor, Adam had only a brief second to react. Alec charged into the open elevator, fists swinging with a rage Adam had never known.

The first few blows landed squarely and powerfully into the side of Adam's head. He raised his arms instinctively to cover his face, and when he did, felt the immeasurable pain from his assailant's foot driving deep into his midsection. With a groan, he fell hard to both knees.

The pain radiated down his legs and his stomach burned. Tears blurred his vision, and blood poured from his mouth. Alec grabbed him by the back of the head, a full patch of hair gripped tightly in his hand.

"So nice to see you again, brother," he said, as he forced Adam's head continually into the side of the elevator. "I would've thought you'd have been more of a challenge than this, Adam. You disappoint me."

Adam fought to hold onto consciousness. A hungry darkness ate at the corner of his vision. Colors as brilliant as any rainbow flashed before him. Worse than the pain though was the realization he was going to die. The frantic awareness that life was so fragile, so prone to the sister's of fate.

He was forced to his feet and pinned to the back of the elevator. The long cold blade of a knife was held flush to his throat. Both his hands gripped Alec's wrist, but he lacked the strength to push it away. Involuntarily, he looked into his brother's eyes. The rage was gone, and in its place a twinkling gleam of satisfaction stared back at him. Adam tried to speak, but was only able to produce a low gurgling sound. Greasy sweat, mixed with his own blood, streamed down his face, into his eyes and mouth, as the darkness moved in.

A paralyzing blow to his ribs sent Adam to the ground again. Coughing and gasping for air, he fought to hold off the darkness that was rapidly overtaking him.

"I was hoping for more of an apocalyptic duel between good and evil, brother. I thought your powers were at least equal to mine, but I see now I overestimated your skills," Alec taunted. "I wanted you to suffer some of the pain and agony you had imposed upon me, but now I know you're too weak and fragile. Your death, no matter how long I drag it out, will be too quick."

He knew Alec was speaking to him, but the words were jumbled, and his concentration began to falter.

"But all is not lost Adam. Perhaps your girlfriend will be able to provide me some entertainment before her death. As a courtesy to you dear, sweet brother, I'll allow you to watch."

Paige.

Adam had all but forgotten she was even in the elevator. He strained to lift his head and in doing so was assaulted with a wave of dizziness and nausea. He closed his eyes tight in an attempt to will away the pain. When he looked up again, he could see her.

She was huddled tightly against the far corner of the elevator. Her eyes were wide with fear and they glistened with unspilled tears. There was no color to her face, just a paleness associated with death, a death that was imminent for them both.

It was his fault. He had unwittingly pulled Paige into his own private hell. Her only crime had been to fall in love with him and now she would pay the ultimate price for those feelings.

Alec touched her cheek, taunting her with words Adam couldn't hear, suggestions he couldn't tolerate. He slowly pulled himself from the floor. His left eye was swollen shut, it hurt to breathe and his ribs were surely broken. However, from somewhere deep inside, from a love he was only recently aware of, Adam seized on a strength few people ever find. An angry, guttural sound came from deep inside his chest as he hurled himself headfirst into Alec. The force caught him by surprise and Alec dropped the knife as they both tumbled into the hallway. They quickly got to their feet and Adam was able to land the first punch, but soon realized he was no match for his brother. The pummeling began again as Adam absorbed blow after angry blow.

Then suddenly Alec fell limp into his arms. To weak to hold him, Adam let his brother fall to the ground and saw the handle of the knife barely protruding from Alec's back. Blood quickly soaking through the shirt and onto the floor, Adam looked up and saw Paige.

Either from fear of her own death, or that of his, Paige had been able to bring herself back from the emptiness which had left her a mere shell.

"Can you make it to the car?" she asked forcefully.

Adam nodded once and let Paige lift his left arm over her right shoulder. She led him from the building and helped him into the passenger seat, then quickly got behind the wheel of the Grand Am. The engine started and Paige wasted no time shifting into gear.

Adam knew he had just taken the worse physical beating of his life. It was a beating that should have left him unconscious, if not dead. However, as he traced the swelling over his left eye, he knew the healing process had already begun. As it was with the bullet wound, his body was quickly repairing any internal damage. He could breathe now without any pain and vision was returning to his left eye. The multiple cuts and wounds he suffered had already stopped bleeding.

Adam was overcome with a sense of awe, a sense of immortality. He wondered if there was anything his body couldn't do and exactly what limitations there were to his newfound power. Just as quickly though, he was overcome with a sense of fear when he thought about Alec lying face down in a puddle of blood. What, if any, were *his* limitations?

CHAPTER *Twenty-Five*

Special Agent Thomas reported to Quinn on the lead and explained it was a hoax. He then listened in false surprise about the attempted kidnapping of Adam MacGregor and his companion. He was informed of Goodwin's delay by local police and as a result they were clueless as to the whereabouts of Adam.

He caught up with his partner at Precinct 12 and together they drove to the Pine Street Inn. Though it was difficult, Rick Goodwin tried to remain optimistic.

"We've got an APB out on both the car and MacGregor. We'll probably have sight of him again within the hour," he said to Thomas.

"I doubt it," Thomas said plainly. "They must know about the Organization or they would have headed straight to the nearest cop. And if they know about the Organization, they're either part of it or smart enough to stay hidden from it."

Goodwin hated to admit when Thomas was right, but he was making sense. The average person would have made a beeline to the nearest police station under the same set of circumstances. Was it possible that Adam MacGregor was part of the Organization, Goodwin wondered? Or was it possible he just stumbled upon more than he could handle? Either way, Goodwin knew it wasn't going to be easy to pick up their trail.

They arrived at the Pine Street Inn just after six o'clock. The nightly dinner crowd was just making their way in and the place looked like a refuge for the walking dead. They made their way to the administration desk and waited patiently for someone to notice them. A middle-aged black man was pushing a mop over an area where hot soup had spilled, and Goodwin approached him.

"Excuse me sir," he said while removing his identification. "My name is Rick Goodwin and I'm with the FBI. Would you mind if I ask you a couple of questions?"

The man looked about nervously and when he saw Thomas approaching, dropped his mop and bolted for the back stairs. Thomas looked in surprise at his partner who was already in pursuit.

Both agents caught up to him easily and stopped him on the second floor landing.

"Whoa, hold on," Thomas said grabbing the man from behind. "What's wrong with you? We only wanted to ask you a few questions about a woman who works here."

The man cursed at himself, then said, "Look, I had nothing do with that guy getting shot, all right? Ms. Allsworth, she just asked me to help her get the guy to one of the vacant rooms and then she sent me to get Doctor Richards, honest. I ain't seen or heard from them since."

The agents looked at each other, realizing what they had stumbled upon.

"What's your name?" Thomas asked.

"Black. Jim Black. Look I's just a janitor here, I don't won't no trouble. You gotta believe me, I had nothing to do with it."

"We know you didn't Mr. Black, all we want is a little assistance. Can you help us out?" Goodwin asked politely.

Still tense and afraid, Black simply nodded.

"Good. Can you take us to where they are?" Goodwin asked.

Again Black nodded and began walking up to the second floor. He took them to the room he had last seen Paige and said, "This is where I left them. Can I go now?"

"In a minute," Thomas said. "Is this the man who was with Allsworth, the one who was shot?" he asked, showing him a recent photograph of Adam.

"Yeah. Yeah, that's him. He was shot in the back. Like I said, I fetched Doctor Richards and after that I ain't seen them. The doctor left about thirty minutes after I fetched him."

Thomas looked at Goodwin as both men pulled out their revolvers.

"OK, get out of here." Thomas said. He knocked twice on the door and identified himself as FBI. When there was no answer, Goodwin kicked in the door.

The room was empty but the rusted smell of dried blood permeated the small area. The bedspreads were covered with red stains and a basin of clouded red water rested on the nightstand.

After thoroughly searching the room for any evidence of where they may have gone, Goodwin removed a cell phone from his pocket and dialed the Boston office of the FBI. While Thomas poked around in the bathroom, Goodwin gave orders to search phone records of any calls coming in or out of the room over the past four hours. He also requested a forensics team and told them to make it a priority.

"He must have taken a bullet back at the townhouse," Goodwin said to Thomas. "By the looks of all this blood, I doubt he'll get too far. We better put an APB out to all hospitals and medical facilities as well."

Thomas nodded in agreement. Returning his revolver to its holster, he said, "I'll check the employee's entrance and try to get statements from anyone who may have seen them come or go. Why don't you see what you can find out from Dr. Richards?"

"All right," Goodwin answered. "We'll meet back here in thirty minutes and see if forensics can come up with anything useful."

Thomas watched as Goodwin retreated back to the main lobby, then he walked the end of the corridor to the employee's entrance. A service elevator was in front of him, but he took the stairs, making a mental note to check the elevator from the ground floor.

He removed a handkerchief from his lapel pocket and carefully opened the access door. If they did come this way, he didn't want to smudge their fingerprints. Out of habit more than concern, he again removed the revolver from its holster and proceeded slowly down the stairs.

He stopped short when he reached the bottom step. There in front of him was the evidence he knew he would find. The wall opposite the door was red stained and streaked. The floor was also covered with a fair amount of blood. Way too much for just one man to lose and still be alive.

He gingerly stepped around the puddles of blood as best he could and pressed the call button to the elevator with his handkerchief. With his gun leveled, the doors slid open to reveal an unoccupied space. The cheap chrome walls and tile floor were literally sprayed and stained with macabre red designs. Again with his handkerchief, he pressed the emergency stop button of the elevator, then noticed the several black and white photographs, now highlighted with blotches of red, lying in the corner next to a shoebox.

He picked one up by its edges and studied the framed antique farmhouse. As he did, a rare smile crossed his face at the sudden realization of what the picture revealed. He placed the photo back in its original position, the awkward grin growing larger. Removing the flip phone from his pocket, he quickly dialed ten digits and waited for the connection.

On the second ring, a cantankerous voice answered.

"Wenzler," the voice said with a low growl.

"It's me," Thomas said pleasantly.

"So," Wenzler barked back.

"So," Thomas answered, "I know where both MacGregor and Alec are headed. And if you want to know, it's going to cost an additional hundred grand."

****

Peter Jones was uncharacteristically short-tempered and moody. He had to learn of the shoot-out at Adam's townhouse from the police scanner, and it had taken his men several hours to get all the details from their varied sources.

Apparently, Adam and a woman identified as Paige Allsworth had managed to escape the scene. Two men, both former police officers, had been killed by FBI agent Rick Goodwin during the shootout. However, neither the police nor the FBI had any clue as to the whereabouts of Adam and Paige, though an all-points bulletin was in effect.

Pacing the makeshift office in downtown Boston, he spoke abruptly with Deputy Director Richard Quinn over the speakerphone.

"And you call a shoot-out in broad daylight, with Adam and the Allsworth woman as hostages, protection. I call it a fuck up!" he said angrily. "And now you tell me you have no idea where they are, where they're headed or even how seriously hurt Adam may be."

Quinn had been the focus of Jones' ire for almost fifteen minutes. Finally, he could take no more. "The FBI is not in existence to serve as your personal babysitter. Our hands have been tied from the very start. You claim to know who Omega is but won't reveal his identity. You claim to know about the inner workings of the Organization, yet you keep us in the dark. You inform us of certain assassinations and violations of federal laws, but do nothing to prevent them. And now you have the audacity to criticize and make judgments about the way my men have performed with little or no information. When we find MacGregor, and we will, he shall be arrested and interrogated like any other fugitive. And if that puts his life at risk, you have no one to blame but yourself. If you want our continued assistance, I suggest you start cooperating more fully. You can start by telling me who the hell you are and who in God's name Omega is."

Silence.

Quinn listened hard and hoped he had not frightened the mystery man away. But he was serious about his threat. He would not subject his men to life and death situations for the benefit of protecting some first-year lawyer without concrete reasons as to why.

After more than thirty years as a federal agent, he was sure he had heard everything a suspect or informant could claim without appearing the least bit surprised. But when Jones finally did speak, the Deputy Director realized how wrong he was.

"Omega is Adam's adoptive father, Neil MacGregor," he began. "Don't bother putting out an APB, you'll never find him. He's dead and buried and not even I know where."

"Jesus, Mary, and Joseph," Quinn whispered, more to himself than to Jones.

"He was killed earlier this afternoon by one of Josef Wenzler's men. Apparently, Omega's concern for his adoptive son outweighed his interest in preserving the Organization, and he paid for it with his life. Quite ironic actually."

Quinn sat motionless for several seconds, then quickly made a feeble attempt to regain his professional composure. "Josef Wenzler? Should I know that name?" he asked, as he scribbled the information into his note pad.

"You should now," Jones said in a deflated tone. "He's running the Organization, and the top item on his agenda is capturing Adam and, as you have already figured out, his brother, Alec."

Quinn sat stunned. He only half-believed the diary of Martin West. The other half of him logically and emotionally discounted the amazing genetic breakthroughs documented in the doctor's diary. He found it difficult to accept that science had somehow improved on God's greatest creation.

Keeping his focus as best he could, Quinn took as many notes as possible, while Jones continued to spill forth all he knew about the Organization. Everything from the perfected DNA sample to Omega's rise in power to the mind altering techniques used on Adam and Alec were at last revealed. He explained the original intent of the

Organization to their now perverse goal of worldwide political domi-
nance. And he informed Quinn of Alec's disappearance and the
Organization's belief that he was hunting Adam. For thirty minutes,
Jones spoke in the same deflated tone, and when he finished, there was
a long silence, as both men contemplated what was at stake.

It was Quinn who finally spoke first, asking the question that had
been bothering him from the start. "And how do you know all this?
Who are you?"

"My alias for twenty-five years has been Peter Jones, but you probably know me by my real name. I'm Doctor Martin West. Adam and Alec
are my sons."

✶✶✶✶✶✶✶✶✶✶✶✶✶✶✶✶✶✶✶✶✶✶✶✶✶✶✶✶✶✶✶✶✶✶

CHAPTER *Twenty-Six*

They parked the Grand Am between a blue Ford pick-up and a yellow Honda Accord in the parking lot of the Golden Palace restaurant. Chinatown was busy on any night of the week and they hoped the crowded parking lot would provide as much cover as possible for their bullet-ridden vehicle. Boston's Red Light district was only a block away and so was their destination.

Adam was still in a state of wonder, as he took one last look at his face in the vanity mirror. His left eye showed only the slightest puffiness, his broken ribs were reduced to a dull ache, and several of the cuts and bruises on his face were no longer visible. Though his injuries were healing remarkably well, his appearance was still frightening and ragged. Dried blood was caked to the sides of his face, chin, and clothing. His shirt and jacket were torn and bloody and he carried with him the repulsive odor of dried sweat mixed with fear.

They purposely left the car unlocked and the keys in the ignition. If someone were desperate enough to steal it, so be it. They would not be returning to the Grand Am, and with any luck, they would be leaving town very shortly with new identities and with different transportation.

As they approached the seedy two-block district, Paige tightened her grasp on Adam's hand.

"Are you sure you know what you're doing?" she asked.

"I'm not sure of anything anymore. But as sad as it may sound, this is our best chance of getting to the farmhouse alive."

"You really know how to instill confidence in a girl, Adam," she said.

They paused briefly, and Adam slid his arms around her waist.

"Paige, I never thanked you for saving my life back at the shelter. Thank you," he said with a soft kiss on her cheek.

"Think nothing of it. I have a feeling you'll be getting a chance to repay me later." She reached up and kissed him tenderly on the lips. "I love you Adam."

He smiled at her and repeated the words. They continued down Washington Street, passing a variety of hookers and drug dealers along with a mixture of businessmen looking for one or the other.

Several decrepit and poorly lit theatres offered first-run pornographic movies, while loud rock and roll music blared from the several adult clubs along the street. The two-block district was a world unto itself. A place where the rules were made up as you went along, and any day could very well be your last.

Finally at the end of the first block, on the corner of Washington Street and Kneeland Street, they came to the Love Hole nightclub.

"First dates are so overrated, don't you think?" Adam smiled nervously at Paige.

"Are you sure this David Green person can get us what we need?" she asked.

"If he can't, he'll know who can."

He pulled open the blackened glass door, as a middle-aged man in a three-piece suit was leaving. The man stared at Adam, then at Paige, before hurrying into the street. Adam was aware of his bloodied face and clothes and just shrugged helplessly at Paige. Once inside, a large, broad-shouldered man asked for identification while eyeing them both suspiciously. Adam pulled out his wallet and showed the man his driver's license.

"I'd like to see David Green, please," Adam said as though they were old friends.

"Nobody here by that name pal. There's a four dollar cover charge, and that goes for the lady too."

Adam didn't want to argue with a doorman and figured once inside they would have a better chance of finding David's office or at least someone who could point them in the right direction. They walked hand in hand passed the glaring stare of the bouncer and into the club. At first, they were blinded by the darkness, then by the neon bulbs and flashing strobe lights. Once their eyes focused, Adam found himself gawking at three incredibly beautiful and very naked dancers. They each held an audience on separate stages and the one in the middle, a blonde with unnaturally large breasts, was violently thrusting her hips into the face of a very sweaty, very grateful man with a handful of dollar bills.

The other two, one on either side of the gyrating big-bosomed blonde, were also entertaining their admirers with several athletic and sexually suggested movements.

"I don't think you'll find David Green up there," Paige said a little annoyed.

Embarrassed, Adam cleared his throat and began to pull Paige through the maze of well-dressed businessmen, rough-looking hoodlums, clean-cut college kids, and skimpily dressed waitresses. Finally reaching the bar opposite the stages, Adam signaled for the burly bartender, and the man lumbered over to them.

He stood at least six feet four and weighed somewhere around three hundred pounds. His beard, knotted and unkempt, hung down to his chest. While one eye glared at Adam, the other wandered aimlessly to the right. For the first time since they escaped the shelter, Paige felt real fear.

"Excuse me sir," Adam said, trying to approach the subject as delicately as possible. He would almost rather have another run in with his brother than with the giant behind the bar. "My friend and I," he said glancing at Paige, "are looking for David Green. Could you tell us where his office is?"

"Who the fuck are you?" the man said loud enough for several of the patrons to hear.

Adam cleared his throat again, feeling the embarrassment burning his cheeks. "I'm his attorney. If you could just tell him Adam MacGregor is here to see him, I'd greatly appreciate it."

The man reached over the bar and grabbed Adam by his already torn jacket. "I ain't never known no attorney to look like some punk who just got his ass kicked in a fight. I don't know who fucked you up, but if you don't get outta my sight and outta this club by the time I count to five, I'm gonna show you what a real beating feels like."

Adam doubted the man could *count* to five but had suffered enough physical abuse for one day. He was about to agree to the man's terms when a voice bellowed from behind him.

"Adam MacGregor! Well I'll be an Uncle Tom," David Green said with genuine surprise and happiness. "Tiny, let my friend go and set him and his girlfriend up with whatever their drinking. On the house, of course."

The bartender grunted once, then reluctantly let go of Adam's jacket. "I'm sorry Mr. Green. I didn't know they was friends of yours," he said humbly, his lazy eye staring at the dim lighting overhead.

"Friends? They're more than friends, Tiny. This man single-handedly kept me out of Walpole State Prison." David leaned into Adam and gave him a bear hug almost as tight as Tiny's grip. "What brings you and the little lady to my find establishment, counselor?"

Trying to regain some of his dignity, he introduced David to Paige, then said, "David we need your help. Is there someplace we can talk?"

"I told you a couple of days ago, Adam, on the steps of the courthouse, I'm a man who repays his debts. Whatever you need, I'm sure I got. Let's go to my office."

✳✳✳✳✳✳✳✳✳✳✳✳✳✳✳✳✳✳✳✳✳✳✳✳✳✳✳✳✳✳✳✳✳✳✳

Alec stood slowly, a dull throb in the center of his back the only indication of his injury. A knife covered with blood rested at his feet. He still felt weak and a bit disorientated from his injury, but there was still work to be done.

Initially, seconds before passing out, he teleported from the shelter into the trash-strewn alley across the street where he first arrived. From where he stood, he could see the flashing blue lights of the police cruisers and the yellow tape surrounding the perimeter of the building.

While unconscious, daylight had been eclipsed by nightfall and the moderate temperatures replaced by a chilling wind. As he watched the activity from behind a Dumpster in the alley, a familiar rage began to overtake him. He thought once he remembered his past and the wickedness of his brother, the emotions that controlled him for so long would finally come under his domain. But he was wrong. He had become aware of a very fundamental truth about himself. Although he eliminated hundreds of people on behalf of the Organization, he knew it as without benefit of choice. Whether it was Adam and his slut companion, or Allison and the men hired to protect her, he needed to kill as a means of satisfying a basic, growing hunger within him.

The fact his brother survived their initial encounter only heightened that need. But his brother was close by. He could feel his presence, sense his fear. The air was heavy with his evil. But there was something even stranger about the sensation.

He could actually see Adam and the bitch in his mind, as clear as if they were standing there before him. He knew exactly where they were, to whom they were talking, and what they were planning. A new, almost psychic power was being born. Whether from their unholy bond of brotherhood or from some untapped source that had remained buried by drugs and experimentation, Alec knew, at a whim, he could teleport to the exact place where Adam had taken refuge.

Smiling to himself, he left he alley and walked past the Pine Street Inn and the several police cruisers parked out front.

✳✳✳✳✳✳✳✳✳✳✳✳✳✳✳✳✳✳✳✳✳✳✳✳✳✳✳✳✳✳✳✳✳✳✳

David led the way, as Adam and Paige followed close behind. A few of the customers gave Paige the once over and smiled approvingly at her. The stares made her uncomfortable, and she held Adam's hand even tighter. The stink of stale beer and whiskey, of layers of cheap perfume, cigarette smoke, and other unidentifiable, but equally offensive smells, combined to make her dizzy and nauseous.

David directed them into the ladies' dressing room and finally through a door hidden behind one of the clothes runners.

"As my attorney, Adam, I assume what you've seen and what we discuss is confidential," David said with a smile.

"Believe me David, I don't want what we discuss to leave these walls anymore than you do."

"In that case," he said opening the door to his office, "have a seat and tell me what I can do for you."

The office was bare and basic and Adam wondered why it was housed in such a secretive location. He half expected to find safes full of money, kilos of cocaine or, at the very least, Jimmy Hoffa playing a game of solitaire. Instead, the office had four dusty, gray walls, three gray folding chairs, a gray filing cabinet, and a gray metal desk.

Adam and Paige sat next to each other on the folding chairs across from David, and Adam began, "To start with David, we need first-rate fake ID's with full back-up, a car that's neither obvious nor hot, and we need a gun that's easy to use and reliable."

David laughed the hardy laugh Adam first heard during their initial meeting at Charles Street Jail. "That's one hell of a Christmas list you have there boy. What happen, you forget to pay your bar dues or something?"

Neither Adam nor Paige smiled at David's apparent joke and when he saw they were serious, the laughter stopped. "Christ sakes boy, you kept me from doing three to five years, you didn't save my life. You have any idea what something like that's gonna cost?"

"I have some cash and plenty of plastic, I'm sure we can work something out."

Again David gave that annoying laugh and said, "Boy, you gotta learn to speak up. Why didn't you say so in the fist place? So how much we talking?"

Adam glanced nervously at Paige then removed his wallet. After a moment, he said, "I have about three hundred in cash and somewhere around eight thousand in credit. Will that get us what we need?"

"Well, that's certainly a good place to start."

David removed a pocket calculator from inside the metal desk and began crunching numbers like a CPA at tax time. After what seemed an eternity, he said, "With my special discount to very special customers, I think we can do business, Adam."

✳✳✳✳✳✳✳✳✳✳✳✳✳✳✳✳✳✳✳✳✳✳✳✳✳✳✳✳✳✳✳✳✳✳✳

CHAPTER *Twenty-Seven*

Alec walked quickly for three blocks with no destination in mind, but with a very specific purpose. The mental images of his prey were still flashing in his mind. He could see them sitting in a gray office somewhere with black man. Soon, very soon, he would be paying them a visit.

Finally, in a part of town he wasn't familiar with, he came upon Wild Bill's Gun and Ammo store. Without pausing, he stepped into the establishment as the bell at the top of the door jingled. A middle-aged man gave him the once over from the counter where he was instructing a young lady on how to use a small Smith and Weston.

"Be with you in a minute, sir," he said with a toothy grin.

Alec nodded and continued scanning the walls and several glass counter-tops. He saw the Glock 9mm pistol, the Mosseberg 12-gauge shotgun, and the Magnum .357, all with the appropriate ammunition in boxes behind the counter. As he studied the arsenal in front of him, his palms began to sweat. However this time, it wasn't from fear. It was from the anticipation of the imminent killing which he was about to conduct.

After about three minutes, the woman thanked the man and turned from the counter. Alec also turned; smiled broadly, then shot her in the head with the handgun tucked in his belt.

Even before the owner could be surprised or scared, Alec turned and fired point blank into his face. The bullet entered just above the bridge of his nose, and for an instant, it appeared as though Wild Bill had a third eye. Alec shuddered with immense pleasure, as the man crumbled to the floor before him. Savoring their deaths for just a moment longer, he quickly smashed the glass counter with his fist and removed the weapons of his choice, loading each with the appropriate ammunition.

Pulling open the door to the street, he turned back to the dead bodies and said, "Have a nice day, folks," then left.

✶✶✶✶✶✶✶✶✶✶✶✶✶✶✶✶✶✶✶✶✶✶✶✶✶✶✶✶✶✶✶✶✶✶✶✶

It had been almost thirty minutes since one of David's cronies entered the office and asked for their height, weight, eye color and preferred alias' before taking their photographs.

While they sat waiting, David ran Adam's credit cards and obtained the full limit on each of them. A total of eight thousand, one hundred and fourteen dollars had been cleared. Adam instinctively flinched each time he signed one of the charge receipts. As if on cue, the crony re-entered the room with a paper bag in each hand just as Adam signed the last receipt.

"Ah, perfect timing Paul. Thank You," David said as the man left without saying a word.

David poured forth the contents in one of the bags and began sifting through them. Handing Adam a license, he said, "Drive safely Robert Phillips. Nice name, you kinda look like a Bob."

Adam took the license and studied it carefully. He couldn't tell it from a real one, though he had no idea how to tell one from the other.

David sensed his thoughts and said, "Guaranteed to stand up to the strictest scrutiny. Of course, the address is phony, but when you get to wherever it is you're going, simply apply for a change of address with the DMV and you're legit."

He then poured the contents of the second bag out and scrambled for another license. Handing it to Paige, he said, "Donna Phillips. Pretty name for such a pretty woman. Congratulations on getting married by the way. I'm a little hurt you didn't invite me, but here's your marriage license nevertheless. All legit."

"I'm impressed David," Adam said. "What else do you have in your bag of tricks?"

With a sheepish smile, he leaned over the desk and handed Adam a set of keys to a 1992 Hyundai. "Best I could do on such short notice, sorry. But hey, it has a full tank of gas. Didn't charge for it either."

"It'll do," Adam said, taking the keys. "Anything else?"

"Just this," he said, removing a gun from his desk drawer. "Very simple, very easy to use. Browning semi-automatic, fully loaded and ready to go." Holding the gun in his hand, he continued, "Flip the safety, aim and shoot. Child's play."

Adam looked at Paige and repeated the words.

"Child's play."

CHAPTER *Twenty-Eight*

Goodwin and Thomas were still at the shelter when the call came in from Officer Jackson of the Boston Police Department. The Grand Am had been located at a restaurant in Chinatown. The car was vacant and the keys were still in the ignition. A discrete, but thorough search of the Golden Palace and the surrounding area had not uncovered the pair of fugitives.

It was just after eight o'clock when Goodwin and Thomas arrived at the scene. A tow truck and three officers were already waiting by the vehicle. There were about ten or fifteen spectators mulling about and a very irate proprietor of the restaurant.

"My customers will start thinking I have broken the law. Please just tow the car and leave my restaurant," an elderly Chinese man was pleading with one of the officers in broken English.

Goodwin flashed his badge and he and Thomas crossed under the yellow tape circling the area.

"You find anything useful," Goodwin asked one of the forensic technicians kneeling beside the passenger door.

"It was them all right," he said. "Her prints are all over the steering wheel and driver's side door, his are on the passenger side. Strange though, we can't find any evidence of wet blood anywhere. The APB said the man was seriously injured."

"Any idea how long the vehicle's been abandoned?" Goodwin asked, peering into the backseat.

"Engine's still warm, and we've located the owner of the white Cadillac parked next to the Grand Am. He says a green pick-up was here when he arrived about an hour ago. He's sure because he remembers he parked too close to the white line and his wife bumped doors when she got out. I'd say no more than forty-five minutes."

Goodwin was about to ask another question when a police sergeant breathlessly interrupted. "Excuse me Agent Goodwin," he began hurriedly, "We've got a positive ID on the MacGregor kid about a block from here. He's in the Red Light District at a club called the Love Hole. A man says he remembers seeing them both go into the club as he was exiting. Says the guy was covered in blood and ripped clothing."

"Let's move," Goodwin hollered. "Sergeant, I want two back-ups at the Love Hole, one in front and one out back. I want to take them both alive and unharmed. I repeat, I want them alive and unharmed. Now let's move!"

"He's coming!" Adam said suddenly without realizing he said it. Both Paige and David mirrored the look of surprise on his face.

"Who's coming?" David asked, as they were about to exit the door of the ladies' dressing room.

The color that had finally returned to Paige's face was gone. In its place was a milky whiteness Adam had become all too familiar with.

"Him? He's found us?" she asked with no attempt to hide her fear.

Adam nodded and removed the Browning semi-automatic from his waistband.

"Whoa," David said quickly. "Are you crazy? You walk out there with a gun pulled and my boys will cut you down before you take one step."

"You don't understand," Adam said, forcing David's hand away from his. "He's coming. Any second now, Alec will be here."

"You should be so lucky," David said with a broad grin. "If this guy you're running from is stupid enough to come in here, especially carrying a gun, your problems just ended. Tiny has a 12-gauge shotgun behind the bar and two of my bodyguards, both adequately armed are close by. Believe me, if your friend wants to start something in my backyard, they'll be carrying his sorry ass outta here in a body bag."

Adam looked at Paige and was about to tuck his gun away when the first shot exploded above the noise of the obnoxiously loud music.

✲✲✲✲✲✲✲✲✲✲✲✲✲✲✲✲✲✲✲✲✲✲✲✲✲✲✲✲✲✲✲✲✲✲✲

Alec was slightly disappointed when his head cleared and his eyes focused on a naked blond rather than Adam. A large hand grabbed him from behind and spun him around.

"Hey pal," the muscular doorman said, "it's a four dollar cover charge."

Alec raised the Mooseberg shotgun from under his jacket and fired once into the man's chest. The doorman was literally lifted from the floor and sent crashing into a table of Japanese businessmen and two underdressed women.

Chaos then erupted as the two women began screaming. Alec turned and through the rushing, scrambling, screaming patrons saw the hill-billy bartender swing toward him with a shotgun of his own.

Alec dove to the left, just as the table he had been in front of a mil-lisecond before exploded into splinters. With the Magnum already in his right hand, Alec rolled onto his stomach and fired once. A hole the size of a baseball appeared in the bartender's chest, but the big man took the impact without falling. Unsteadily, the bartender aimed the shotgun again, this time blowing out the mirrored wall that Alec was pressed against.

The second hole, just as large and red as the first, opened the bar-tender's throat sending him backward into shelves of liquor and glasses.

With the Magnum still in one hand and the Glock semi-automatic in the other, Alec stayed close to the wall as screaming women and panicked men tried to find a door or window to escape through. The continuous pounding of the rock and roll music coupled with the surrounding confusion made it difficult for him to focus on Adam's whereabouts.

He started away from the wall just as the bullet entered his left thigh. A second bullet, coming from behind the stage, grazed his left ear and splintered the doorway to the men's room.

Grabbing a naked redhead with spiked heels as she tried to flee, Alec pulled her in front of the line of fire. A third bullet coming from a different direction drilled the redhead's right breast and left her limp in his arms.

Alec began firing both weapons in the general direction of the stage. Several men and women fell to the ground as bullets punctured various parts of their bodies.

He needed cover and time to assess the trap his brother had set for him. Once again, he underestimated the cleverness of Adam's wicked ways. Stepping over the dead redhead, Alec lunged into the men's room directly behind him.

****

David, Adam and Paige eased open the door to the ladies' dressing room just in time to see Tiny take the second bullet to the throat.

"Jesus," David said, as he pulled the door shut. "Follow me!"

Pushing past the stunned pair, David went back toward his office. "Hurry!" he yelled, glancing over his shoulder.

Adam had to physically pull Paige away from the door. He was sure she was going to slip back into her semi-self at any minute, but she quickly snapped out of it and followed close behind.

Rather than turning into his office, David led them through a dimly lit corridor. The floor was wet, and the offensive odor of sewerage clung to the air.

"It's not pleasant, but it beats going out the front door," David said breathlessly, pulling open a trap door in the ceiling. A pair of rotted stairs came down and he looked earnestly at Adam. "This is where we part company my friend. I ain't never seen or heard from you since the day of my hearing. Now get outta here."

Adam looked up into the hole and saw nothing but blackness. The sound of running water echoed from somewhere above and the stench of sewer got worse.

"Where exactly are you sending us?" Adam asked.

"It's a crawl space that runs adjacent to the sewer pipes. About thirty yards down is another trap door that leads to the roof. From there you can take the fire escape to street level. Your car is parked about half a block up on Kneeland Street. Now hurry, for God's sake. Adam you go first in case there are rats hanging around up there."

Adam shook David's hand and thanked him before climbing up the stairs and disappearing into the blackness. Paige paused, then hugged David. "Thank you," she said sincerely.

"You take care of that boy now, you hear. I'm probably gonna need a good lawyer real soon," he said with a smile.

✶✶✶✶✶✶✶✶✶✶✶✶✶✶✶✶✶✶✶✶✶✶✶✶✶✶✶✶✶✶✶✶✶✶✶✶

CHAPTER *Twenty-Nine*

After a forty-five minute standoff, the FBI and the Boston SWAT team stormed the men's room of the Love Hole and, to their chagrin and slight embarrassment, found it unoccupied.

The Glock 9mm pistol and Mooseberg 12-gauge shotgun were found in the corner next to the urinals. A river of blood trailed from the door to the back wall, but gave no indication as to how the man escaped.

Thirteen people were dead and eight seriously wounded. From the dozen or so witnesses that were still alive and came forward, a positive ID had been made on the gunman.

A second APB had been issued for Adam MacGregor, this time listing thirteen counts of first-degree murder. The words, "considered armed and dangerous," were also added to Adam's description. Roadblocks had been set up on all streets leading out of town, and a door-to-door search was underway. The forty-five minute delay outside the men's room though made the prospects of finding Adam dubious at best.

Goodwin and Thomas sat with David Green in his small gray office.

"Mr. Green, we can do this here or downtown, the choice is yours," Goodwin said. "We know Adam MacGregor was your attorney, and we know that he was here tonight. What we don't know is why?"

"I told you bastards I'm not talking without my lawyer present. I've been around the block enough to know my rights. You ain't got nothing on me."

Goodwin stood abruptly and leaned into David. "I'll tell you what we have on you Green. You're an accessory after the fact and quite possibly before. You're obstructing justice and interfering with a Federal investigation. There are thirteen dead bodies in a club you own, not to mention the stash of illegal firearms found in your basement. And you're a three-time loser. Don't think for a minute we can't nail you for at least a half dozen felonies. With your track record, you can thank God Massachusetts doesn't have the death penalty. Now you can either cooperate with us and save yourself a shitload of unnecessary headaches or we can lock you up now and throw away the key. Your choice."

Thomas watched nervously from behind Goodwin. He didn't need to know what name MacGregor was using or what car he was driving or what plans he had confided in Green. None of that mattered to Thomas. He already knew where MacGregor was headed, and it was in his best interest that Adam arrive before being apprehended. A great deal of money was at stake, and he'd be damned if he allowed a scum like Green to jeopardize it.

"OK, OK. Don't go playing Elliot Ness with me. If I tell you what I know, I've got your word you won't involve me?" David asked nervously. He liked Adam, but he liked his freedom much more.

"We're not interested in you Green. Just tell us what you know about Adam," Goodwin said harshly.

"Fuck it then. He didn't tell me where he was headed, I didn't ask. Just said he had to go underground for a while and needed some fake paper. He's going by the name of Robert Phillips. Him and his girlfriend are driving a 92 Hyundai, Massachusetts plates, number 231-OLP. They left while that crazy mother-fucker was shooting up my club. That's all I know," Green said.

Goodwin had been scribbling the information in his note pad. When Green finished, he handed the paper to Thomas.

"Call this in," he said to his partner. "Figure he's been on the road for an hour, so give him a seventy-five mile radius."

Thomas took the paper and walked past Goodwin to where Green was sitting. "How do we know he's telling the truth?" he asked, while removing his revolver.

"Instinct," Goodwin said. "Now move."

"My instinct says he's telling the truth too. Which is unfortunate." Pointing the gun at Goodwin, he fired it once into the chest of his partner. The impact of the slug at close range sent him toppling over backward onto the floor. Turning to Green, he removed another revolver from his belt and said, "Big mouth," and shot him in the head.

Before the SWAT team could respond to the shots, Thomas placed the revolver he killed his partner with into the palm of David Green. Then, quite casually, he knelt beside Goodwin and pretended to perform CPR while he waited for the officers to arrive.

✳✳✳✳✳✳✳✳✳✳✳✳✳✳✳✳✳✳✳✳✳✳✳✳✳✳✳✳✳✳✳✳✳✳✳✳

Dr. Martin West faxed Quinn the list of all known and suspected agents converted by the Organization. He confided in Quinn about his attempts to quicken Adam's recall, first by meeting him, then by delivering to Paige pictures of the boys as children, along with photographs of the farmhouse in which Adam once lived.

"I'm afraid I may have done more harm than good," West said, almost apologetically.

"Why did you wait until now to try and make contact? Surely there must have been other opportunities in the past twenty-five years?" Quinn asked.

'The Organization is very deep. If I had come out of hiding and tried to make contact with Adam, they would've killed us both. When my sources within the Organization informed me of Alec's emotional outbursts and uncontrollable rage, I knew immediately what was happening. And I knew that if Alec was experiencing a memory collapse, Adam would be also. My only chance was to wait until it happened and be there when it did. I've had Adam followed for almost a year now."

Quinn could feel the pain in West's voice. To have a son raised by the man who tried to kill you must have been unbearable. To be so close as to touch him, but so far you couldn't risk being in the same block as him must have been a living hell. Quinn felt enormous pity for Dr. West. Wanting to change the topic for both their sakes, he began flipping through the pages of names West sent over.

"This fax you sent me has one hundred and thirty-seven FBI agents listed, including the Director. Tomorrow morning, the Justice Department shall issue one hundred and thirty-six arrest warrants. I'll deliver the Director's personally," he said, as he studied the names. On the third page, his eyes went wide and his blood turned cold.

"Shit!" he said into the phone.

"What is it?" West asked quickly. "What's the matter?"

"On page three you have listed Special Agent Bob Thomas. Are you sure about him?" Quinn asked, as he was already picking up a second phone.

"Absolutely," West said. "As a matter of fact, sources tell me he's the one who killed Omega. Why?"

The second phone was already ringing, and before he could answer West, a man picked up the car phone receiver.

"Thomas here," he said.

"Bob, it's Quinn. Let me speak to Rick."

Thomas paused momentarily, then said, "Sir, I'm sorry to have to tell you this, Rick Goodwin was killed about ten minutes ago in the line of duty. MacGregor escaped, and we have no idea where he's headed or what he's driving. I'm afraid we've come to a dead end."

****

Adam and Paige safely had eluded the police and more importantly Alec. When they reached the roof of the Love Hole, the scene below them was even more confused and chaotic than the massacre inside. The other strip clubs emptied at the sounds of so many police cruisers and ambulances. Men and women were running helter-skelter from the Love Hole and SWAT teams and local police were jockeying for position around the building. It had been easy for them to climb down the fire escape and vanish into the multitude of chaos.

As Adam drove southbound on Route 95 toward upstate New York, more and more of his past became clear. There was no doubt Alec was his twin brother. Memories of the sadistic experiments they endured as children and of the growing hatred and distrust between them were unfolding even as he drove.

Images of his parents, mostly his mother, brought a painful sense of loneliness and isolation. His mother was a beautiful, compassionate woman. He could almost feel her warmth and love even now. The way she would hold him and sing to him after one of the bizarre experiments had failed. The way she would call him her little Einstein and make such a big deal about his advanced intelligence. Most of all, Adam could remember how very much he loved her.

His father's image was a little cloudier, but he was still able to hold onto small fragments of the man. He was familiar in other ways also, ways in which his subconscious had yet to reveal. Adam knew if he could stay alive long enough to make it to the farmhouse, he would be able to recall everything about his biological father.

The farmhouse was the key though. Even without the map or the photos, he knew exactly where he was headed. The building belonged to his grandmother, although the woman was simply a caretaker and not really related. She was an evil woman who despised him as a child. The farmhouse had also been the last time he had seen his brother. The last time Alec tried to kill him. Adam now knew the significance of his most troubling nightmare. It was Alec who started the fire in hopes of catching him in his room. Instead, it had been his grandmother's unfortunate fate to be inspecting the attic on that morning.

There was one more deeply troubling aspect of the farmhouse. As the revelation suddenly dawned on him, he almost lost control of the car.

"Adam, be careful," Paige yelled, as the car swerved onto the shoulder of the highway. "Are you all right?"

Adam slowed the car down and stopped in the breakdown lane.

"The farmhouse," he said without looking at Paige.

"What about it?" she asked.

Shaking his head slowly in disbelief, he said, "The farmhouse belonged to Mac. I can remember him taking me there several times as a child. On the ride from the facility to the farm, we used to sing Old MacGregor had a farm. Only I was too young to pronounce all the words correctly. My version came out as Omega had a farm." He looked at Paige and knew immediately she understood the implication. "Mac is Omega, and I gave him the name."

They were silent for several moments before Paige leaned over the console and hugged him. "I know what it feels like to find out your father's not the person you think he is. I'm sorry for you Adam."

The embrace ended with a tender kiss, and when Paige pulled away, her face showed a different emotion. "Adam, how did Alec know we were at the club tonight? How did he find us so quickly?"

"Alec has many abilities I don't pretend to understand, Paige. But I think he has some sort of psychic connection with me. The same way I was able to sense him approaching, he must've been able to sense where we were."

"Does that mean he knows where we are now?"

"I think so, though I'm not sensing him anywhere near us."

"Maybe he's dead. Maybe he was killed back at David's club," Paige said without much conviction.

Adam shook his head. "There's no sense in even considering that possibility. We both know he's alive, and we both know we'll see him again, probably at the farmhouse. It's best if we accept that now and prepare for the confrontation."

Paige agreed and pulled the Browning semi-automatic from her purse. "I just hope there's some way he can be killed."

****

CHAPTER *Thirty*

Thomas played the role of the grieved partner and gave his statement several times to the local police and to fellow FBI agents.

While under interrogation by Goodwin and himself, Green pulled a gun from somewhere under his desk and shot Goodwin in the chest. Before he could duplicate the feat, Thomas shot the suspect once in the head. A further search of the hidden corridor uncovered a trap door that led to the roof. No doubt it was how Green planned to escape.

Thomas left the crime scene about ten-thirty and drove immediately to Interstate 95. Adam and Paige already had a two-hour head start, and his map indicated the farmhouse was a three-and-a-half hour drive.

He was sure Wenzler and his men were already in place, waiting for their guests to arrive. The doctor told him his money would be delivered upon the successful capture of Adam, and he wanted to be there to collect in person. It wasn't that he didn't trust Wenzler; he just didn't trust anybody who was holding five hundred thousand dollars of his money.

A flight to South America had already been booked for tomorrow morning and by tomorrow evening, he would begin living the good life. The FBI, Quinn, Adam, Alec, and Wenzler could all kiss his ass good bye. He was going to be a self-made man, and all he needed to do was make certain MacGregor arrived safely at the farmhouse.

Entering onto the Interstate, Thomas pushed the speedometer to eighty-five and hit the cruise control. For the remainder of the drive, he entertained visions of lazy sunsets and frozen Pina Coladas.

* *

Alec found himself back in the trash-strewn alley across the street from the Pine Street Inn. It was the third time he teleported to that location in one day, the last two times while on the brink of unconsciousness. Apparently, it was the easiest location for him to fix onto and one he was now familiar with.

He cursed silently to himself, as he ran a finger over the clotted blood on his left ear. Another half an inch and even his extraordinary metabolism would have been no match for a head injury of that magnitude. He had to be more careful. His brother was obviously deceptive and more clever than he first thought. Adam had somehow been able to lull him into another trap. Though he was angry, the familiar rage was absent, and he knew why. The immeasurable thrill and satisfaction of killing so many people in such a short span of time. He shivered with an almost religious fervor when he relived the excitement of pulling the naked redhead into the line of fire and feeling her struggling body go limp as the bullet ripped open her chest. Hearing the screams of terror as bullets sprayed the strip club. Seeing blood at almost every turn. The smell of burnt powder as a variety of different gunfire erupted. It was all so exciting and wonderful.

He closed his eyes for a moment to relieve the incredible sensations, but instead saw Adam and the girl. They were in a car, pulled over to the side of the road.

On the run again, he thought.

He watched, as Adam put the small Hyundai in gear and re-entered the highway. He knew where they were going. His psychic bond with his brother was getting stronger by the minute.

Upstate New York.

A farmhouse.

The farmhouse.

The one in which he had tried to kill Adam as a child. The one that he burnt, as the old lady frantically fought to escape.

It was a place of evil. A place where Adam had first taken refuge. It was only fitting that the climax to their struggle be decided there.

He would wait until they arrived before he made his appearance. He didn't know the extent of his brother's power, but this time he would not rush into a trap. He would wait and be prepared.

In the meantime though, he again closed his eyes and began to shutter at the images of so much bloodshed and death all around him. If a man could experience the ultimate satisfaction, the ultimate sense of life, Alec believed he found the way.

✱✱✱✱✱✱✱✱✱✱✱✱✱✱✱✱✱✱✱✱✱✱✱✱✱✱✱✱✱✱✱✱✱✱✱

It was just after one o'clock in the morning when Adam pulled off the small country road and onto a dirt path somewhere in Gloversville, New York.

Paige had unwillingly given into sleep, and Adam caught himself smiling, as he watched her angelic bliss. He hated to wake her, but needed her alert for whatever lay ahead. Gently, he nudged her shoulder until she woke with a start.

"It's all right, sweetheart. It's me," Adam whispered quietly. "The farmhouse is about a mile down this road. I think from this point on we should expect the unexpected."

"Have you remembered anything else?" she asked, as she sat up straight.

"Just bits and pieces. I remember a demented vile old doctor named Josef Wenzler. He was the one in charge of the experiments. I can remember him and my mother fighting all the time about the severity of his tests. He used to tell her that Alec and I weren't human and were created for the sole purpose of the Organization. The scary thing was, I think he really believed that."

"Adam, I've been thinking," Paige said. "There must be some members of the Organization who want you to remember and end the

Organization's reign of terror. Somebody in the group had to send me those photos and the map of this place."

Adam agreed, but kept to himself his suspicions about whom he thought responsible. Turning on his high beams, he slowly maneuvered the vehicle over the poorly graveled road toward their final destination.

✶✶✶✶✶✶✶✶✶✶✶✶✶✶✶✶✶✶✶✶✶✶✶✶✶✶✶✶✶✶✶✶✶✶✶✶

CHAPTER *Thirty-One*

"The prodigal son returns," Wenzler said softly.

At the picture window, he and two others watched the Hyundai through infrared goggles as it headed toward the farmhouse from the only viable entrance. Outside, a dozen men were positioned around the property. Some safely hidden atop a small hill to the left of the building, others behind the decrepit barn out back, and still others in the woods about a hundred yards from the house. Once Adam and the woman were trapped inside, the men would close the perimeter preventing any escape. They could not afford to miss this chance to recapture Alec. The future of the Organization would be decided in the next couple of hours.

After receiving the phone call from Thomas earlier in the day, Wenzler and his men drove directly to the farmhouse in upstate New York, arriving just after seven o'clock.

He hadn't been to the property since the day Alec tried to burn it to the ground. Looking upon it now, some twenty-five years later, nothing about it seemed changed. Each slope and curve of land, each building, each tree, appeared as he remembered them from a distant time. The main structure was dark and ominous. The fire had blackened the top two floors of the three-story farmhouse. A large empty space, where the top floor and ceiling had been, now served as home to much of nature's wildlife.

Wenzler strategically deployed his field teams, and then he and two others went inside to await Adam's arrival. The front door was locked, but easily jimmied by one of the men. There was no electricity or heat, just as there hadn't been for twenty-five years.

The foyer was covered in age-old ash, dirt and debris. A medieval knight in full armor holding a large battle-ax stood guard in a lonely corner. Most of the original furniture had remained in the house and by now had molded sufficiently to omit a terribly stale odor.

"Alec can't be far behind now," Wenzler said with an air of anticipation. "Remember, no matter what, Adam is to be taken alive. He's the only bait we have in luring Alec here."

✶✶✶✶✶✶✶✶✶✶✶✶✶✶✶✶✶✶✶✶✶✶✶✶✶✶✶✶✶✶✶✶✶✶✶✶

The high beams of the Hyundai, coupled with the radiance of a full moon, adequately illuminated the vast expanse of the farmhouse and its several acres of maples, birches and pine trees. In another memory, a memory manufactured for him by the Organization, these were beautiful, majestic acres. In that memory, Adam had been especially fond of the farmhouse in wintertime. By day, it was a magical land of whiteness, of snow forts and of sledding with friends. On clear, crisp nights, there were more stars than were humanly possible to count, and the blackness of night was eternal.

But now with his true identity crashing through, Adam couldn't help feel it was the ugliest place on earth. A place of unspeakable horrors, filled only with unpleasant memories. A place malformed by nature and gnarled by disease. The house, the barns, and the stables looked haunted and menacing, looming as gracelessly as open graves in the eeriest of cemeteries.

He didn't want to be here. He wanted desperately to throw the little Hyundai into reverse and drive as fast and as far as he could. He wanted to start over with his new identity in the most remote corner of the earth and put it all behind him. But he knew he couldn't. His destiny was somehow inextricably linked to whatever lay within the farmhouse.

"Should we go in now or wait for the morning light?" Paige asked.

Adam's heart pounded. His mouth was so dry it was difficult to swallow, and his palms too sweaty to sufficiently grip the steering wheel. Nevertheless, he looked at Paige and said with conviction, "Now."

****

They were standing in the foyer, the Halogen flashlight taking in the entire hallway. The lonely guard of armor stood quietly in his corner, unwilling and unable to reveal any of his secrets. The musty smell of decay filled their nostrils. They looked at each other for a moment; both tentatively clutching their Browning semi-automatic's which David had supplied.

"Is anything else coming back?" Paige whispered.

Adam simply shook his head, as he scanned the room with his flashlight.

"No," he said pointing with a beam of light. "Up there is where my bedroom was. From outside I could see Alec grinning at me while the house and my grandmother burned."

"Is Alec here now?" she asked nervously.

"I don't think so. At least I don't feel him."

They walked from the foyer into what was the living room. The light scanned the fireplace, some old furniture, several cobwebs, but nothing that caused any revelations. They were about to leave the living room when the beam caught a portrait of a man and a woman hanging above the fireplace. The woman was very beautiful, with olive skin and jet black hair. She was young, maybe in her late twenties or early thirties, and an air of sophistication lent itself to the image. The man was roughly the same age and had that same intelligent aura to his face. His eyes were ice blue and seemed to penetrate the canvas and stare deeply into Adam's soul. Suddenly Adam knew not only who they were, but also who he was.

"Those are my parents, Paige. I know they are. That's Dr. Martin West and his wife Dr. Jane West. But I don't remember that portrait being here when I was a child. I know for a fact that it wasn't."

As Paige studied the faces in the portrait, she tightened her grip on Adam's arm. "Adam, do you know who that man looks like?" she asked with disbelief.

Adam didn't say anything for a long minute, then said calmly, "My father's alive, Paige. Peter Jones is my father."

Before he could register the surprise on her face, the silence was interrupted by the sound of air escaping a vacuum.

Adam fell to the floor the same instant as Paige, and the last thing he saw was Peter Jones' ice-blue eyes staring down from the portrait.

"Put them both on the couch. The drug should wear off in about an hour or so," Wenzler said, as he walked directly to the fireplace. "So, Martin West is alive after all."

✶✶✶✶✶✶✶✶✶✶✶✶✶✶✶✶✶✶✶✶✶✶✶✶✶✶✶✶✶✶✶✶✶✶✶✶✶

CHAPTER *Thirty-Two*

Thomas pulled onto the dirt path leading to the farmhouse just after four in the morning. He had driven aimlessly for an hour and a half in search of the small dirt path and finally found it by accident when he pulled over to answer nature's call.

Two men with modified Uzi's stopped his car and dragged him onto the road. After notifying Wenzler of the man's identity, Thomas was allowed access to the farmhouse.

"What the hell are you doing here?" Wenzler said, annoyed by the intrusion.

"We had a deal. Once you captured MacGregor, I got my money," Thomas said boldly. "And," he added looking at the unconscious bodies on the couch, "I see my information proved correct."

"Yes Thomas, you have been very helpful. The Organization is indebted to you."

"To the tune of a half million dollars," Thomas added.

"The money's in the BMW. It would be too risky to try and get it now. We're expecting a very important visitor, and any unnatural movement could frighten him away. So I'm afraid you're going to have to wait a few more hours for your reward."

"I have a flight in three hours, and God only knows how long it's going to take me to find my way out of this hellhole. Just give me my money and let me get the fuck out of here," he said angrily.

Wenzler glared at Thomas a moment, then turned to one of his men. "If this asshole says another word, shoot him."

Thomas' jaw dropped, but no words came out.

****

The rage and humiliation were almost unbearable. Alec couldn't believe the vision he witnessed through his psychic sense. Wenzler and Adam were together at the farmhouse. A dozen heavily armed men were hidden around the property in an attempt to protect Adam.

Another trap, but this time Adam had turned the Organization against him. He was now the one being hunted. He was now the one the Organization wanted killed or captured. His brother's evil had manipulated the people Alec trusted most. He would have to kill them all. He would have to carry on the work of the Organization alone. No one could be trusted.

As morning light first began to rise over the plains and valleys of upstate New York, Alec transported deep into the wooded cover of the farmhouse. Without actually seeing them, he knew two men were hidden in a grassy knoll thirty yards to his left. He'd lost his weapons back at the nightclub and had not been able to replace them. He would therefore be forced to resort to his martial arts training. The element of surprise being his best ally.

On his belly, he crawled slowly and deftly toward the men. Ten yards from their position, he watched anxiously, as one of them stood and walked behind a tree to relive himself.

In an instant, Alec snapped the man's neck like a twig, and he fell limply to the ground with his penis still in his hand. He removed the micro Uzi from the dead man's shoulder and a hunting knife from a strap inside his boot.

The other traitor was still lying face down, peering at the road through high-powered binoculars. Throwing the Uzi over his own shoulder, he gripped the knife and rushed toward the second man. The blade cut deeply across his neck, slicing open the aorta and nearly severing his head. Again Alec shuddered from pure ecstasy.

With three more men in the barn, two in the woods and four more at the entrance to the dirt road, Alec closed his eyes and teleported again.

✳✳✳✳✳✳✳✳✳✳✳✳✳✳✳✳✳✳✳✳✳✳✳✳✳✳✳✳✳✳✳✳✳✳

CHAPTER *Thirty-Three*

"He's coming!" Adam shouted, as he woke from his drug-induced sleep. "He's coming!"

He and Paige were propped on a couch, Wenzler sitting across from them and three men standing directly behind the doctor.

Thomas was the first to move toward the picture window. With sunrise illuminating the landscape, he scanned the yard, the barn, and the stables, but saw nothing.

"Is Alec here?" Paige whispered to Adam.

"He's outside," he answered with difficulty.

Wenzler removed a hand-held radio from his hip and said briskly, "All units report."

Silence.

"This is Wenzler. Blue team report."

Silence.

"Red team."

The worried looks passed between Wenzler and the members of his team. "Montgomery," he said sharply, "you and Wilson recon the area. Find out what's going on and report back to me. Take the tranquilizer guns. If Alec is here, I don't want him injured."

"He's here," Adam said softly. "He's here."

* * * * * * * * * * * * * * * * *

Alec watched, as two men left the farmhouse and headed off in different directions. All twelve of the men on the outside had been killed easily, and once he took care of these two, he would visit with the traitorous Wenzler and his evil brother.

One of the men was tentatively inspecting the area behind the barn and was about to speak into a hand-held radio when Alec grabbed him from behind. Swinging the man around, he plunged the hunting knife deep into his chest, savoring the sound of ripping flesh and the sensation of warm blood gushing over his hands. The wide-eyed horror of the man's final seconds alive added to his pleasure.

The second man was kneeling behind the grassy knoll where Alec first teleported and had made his initial kill. Again he closed his eyes and pictured the spot in his mind.

"Doctor, this is Wilson," the man said into his radio. "I'm behind the grassy knoll, and both members of the green team are dead. It looks like Williams had his neck snapped, and Jackson's throat has been cut wide open."

"What about Alec? Is there any sign of him?" Wenzler said over the static.

A gunshot echoed loudly through the radio. Wenzler was about to speak, but before he could, the radio came to life again.

"I'm right here Doctor," Alec said. "There's no need to come looking for me, I'll find you."

****

CHAPTER *Thirty-Four*

Thomas and Wenzler forced Adam and Paige at gunpoint up the ancient stairway and into the master bedroom.

"Let's just give him MacGregor for Christ sakes, if that's all he wants," Thomas said, as he checked the bullets in his revolver.

"Shut up you fool. He thinks he's been betrayed. He's going to try and kill all of us if we don't stop him. MacGregor is our only hope. As long as he's alive and with us, Alec's initial reaction will be to kill him first. It will be our only chance to subdue him."

"You mean kill him, don't you Doctor?"

"No, subdue him, with these high-powered tranquilizer guns. He mustn't be killed. He's the last link to the Organization's glory. Do you understand me Thomas? Subdue him!"

"He's coming," Adam involuntarily said again. This time though, with much more urgency to his voice.

"No shit asshole," Thomas responded angrily. "I still say we just give him MacGregor and the girl and get the fuck out of here."

Before Wenzler could chastise him again, Thomas fell forward face first and lay motionless, a large hunting knife protruding from the nape of his neck. Standing behind him, Alec smiled at his three remaining enemies.

"Alec!" Wenzler pleaded. "Alec, it's me, Dr. Wenzler. I'm your friend. You see I captured Adam for you. I brought him here for you to destroy," he said, as he inched closer to the tranquilizer gun.

Alec didn't hear a word. The rage building inside had him reached a boiling point, and he charged at Wenzler. Picking the man up off the floor, he pinned him against the wall. Both hands wrapped tightly around his neck, and Wenzler fought desperately for air.

"I gave my life to you Doctor. I gave it to Omega and the Organization. I'm the one who deserved your love and devotion. Not him!" Alec said in a fury of hatred.

With his face and eyes beginning to bulge ever so slightly, Wenzler could only gasp for another breath.

"Go!" Adam said, pushing Paige from the bed.

She rushed out of the bedroom and raced down the stairs. Reaching the front door, she turned just as Alec crashed into Adam at the head of the steps. The fall carried them down the flight of stairs, tumbling one on top of the other.

They reached the dirt-covered foyer in unison, their momentum carrying them into the knight of armor still guarding his corner. The battle-ax was jarred loose, digging its still sharp blade into the creaking floorboard inches from Adam's head.

Alec got to his feet quickly, showing no apparent pain from his daring leap of a moment ago. He pulled Adam up by his hair and drove his own forehead into Adam's. A deep red gash immediately appeared, and Adam fell back to the ground.

There would be no second chances this time. There would be no miracle rescues or hidden gunmen to save Adam. This time he would make it quick and do it right.

Pulling out the hunting knife he retrieved from Thomas' neck, he straddled Adam's chest and raised the blade high over head. Adam grabbed his brother's arm at the elbow and, with what little strength he had left, fought to keep the knife away from his throat.

But it was a losing battle. Slowly, steadily, the knife moved closer and closer to his neck. Their eyes locked onto one another and held firm. Alec's pale blue eyes shimmered with excitement while Adam's eyes reflected only fear and panic. Closer and closer the cold steel of the blade pushed toward its desired target, until Adam could feel the tip pressed against his throat.

"No last words, brother. No parting remarks before I cut your black heart from your chest," Alec said through clenched teeth. "It wasn't enough for you to turn our parents against me. No, you weren't going to be satisfied till you had them all betray me."

It was over. Staring up at the identical reflection of himself, Adam knew he was about to die. Images quickly passed before him as the first traces of blood trickled down his neck.

There was Mac teaching him the proper technique in hooking a bass and throwing a baseball. The countless times they sat together, while Mac would patiently explain the intricacies of Constitutional law, or Adam would talk about a new girl that had caught his eye. The night he met Allison Allsworth and being sure he had just been introduced to the most beautiful woman in the world. The long conversations he'd had with Paige, all the time thinking she could very well be the kindest, most intelligent woman he'd ever met. Friends at Yale, passing the bar, discovering the identity of Omega, and the realization he had met his biological father and never knew it, flooded from his memory.

He was close to surrendering his will. The dark edges of sleep were closing in on him. Alec was still smiling; also sensing the end was near.

Suddenly, Alec was gone. The face, the smile, the blueness of his eyes simply vanished before him. At first, Adam though he'd passed out, but he could still feel the physical weight of Alec on his chest. The pressure to his neck and the pointed blade of the knife no longer a hindrance, Adam forced his head from the ground.

Standing before him, Paige looked horrified and sickened. She held the blood-soaked battle-ax limply in her hands, her eyes fixed to an object on the floor beside Adam. When he followed her line of vision, he let out an involuntary gasp at the severed head of Alec lying beside him. His brother's eyes were still wide open and the terrible smile was forever frozen to his face.

Several minutes seemed to pass, as they stared in frightened disbelief. When she was sure the head wouldn't miraculously reattach itself to its missing body, Paige dropped the ax and fell to her knees. Pushing the remains of Alec's body off his chest, Adam crawled over to her and tightly held her in his arms.

"It's over, sweetheart. It's over," Adam said softly.

He wasn't sure she could hear him over the muffled sobs. With her face buried deeply in her hands, Adam gently rocked her.

He was about to say something else to her, when two gun shots erupted next to them, and Dr. Wenzler tumbled down the flight of stairs, the Browning semi-automatic close behind.

They stared at the foyer where Peter Jones stood, his own gun following the path of the dead doctor. Behind him, Adam recognized the Deputy Director of the FBI, Richard Quinn.

✳✳✳✳✳✳✳✳✳✳✳✳✳✳✳✳✳✳✳✳✳✳✳✳✳✳✳✳✳✳✳✳✳✳

CHAPTER *Thirty-Five*

Dr. Martin West and his son, Adam, talked in private for almost an hour. When Quinn and Paige finally entered the room, they saw the two men hugging one another tightly. Neither of the men made any attempt to hide their tears.

The four of them settled uneasily onto the dusty old furniture, then Adam and Paige recounted to the Deputy Director their ordeal over the last three days. They sat in silence while the Deputy Director reviewed his notes.

Finally, Quinn stood. "The way I see it," he began, "Adam MacGregor died here last night. Family members and fingerprints positively identified his severed head and body. Mr. Jones here never existed as far as I'm concerned. Bob and Donna Phillips disappeared and were never heard from again."

Adam genuinely smiled for the first time in days, as he realized what Quinn was saying.

"Adam and I are free to go then?" Paige asked hesitantly.

"No, he's not," Quinn said, pointing at Adam. "Like I said, Ms. Allsworth, Adam MacGregor was killed here last night. I have no objection though, if Bob and Donna Phillips were to leave. And if I were them, I'd leave immediately, before the press and TV cameras arrived."

"Where would we go?" Adam asked. "We have no money. We're driving a stolen car, and obviously if Adam MacGregor is dead, we can't go back to my townhouse or anywhere else I might be recognized."

"Have you ever been to Wyoming?" Martin West asked from the corner of the musty room.

"Wyoming? No, I can't say I have. How about you Donna?"

Paige shook her head, still confused about what was happening.

"Well, I own seventy acres of the prettiest farmland you've ever seen. I've lived there off and on for the last twenty-five years. It's safe and it's anonymous. If you like, I'd be honored to have you both live with me."

They smiled, and Adam said, "It would be us who would be honored, sir."

They were about to leave when Quinn said, "Mr. Phillips, don't forget your suitcase."

"That's not mine, sir. I've never seen it before."

"Trust me Bob. It's yours."

Opening the luggage, Adam stared in amazement at the stacks of hundred dollar bills. "I assume it was to be Thomas' pay-off," Quinn said. "But I've never seen it. Take it and go."

Epilogue

"Sweetheart," Donna Phillips whispered softly in her husband's ear. "The children are waiting for us."

Adam, known by neighbors and friends the past five years as Bob Phillips, rolled onto his back and smiled up at Paige.

"Where do they get all their energy?" he said groggily.

Three years ago, Paige had given birth to a set of very healthy twin boys, Martin and Robert, named after their grandfathers.

"They've been up for hours already," Paige said. "Your father's taking them horseback riding down by the river."

"Christ, where does dad get all *his* energy."

He pulled her close to his naked body and said with a devilish grin, "Where did you get all your energy last night?"

She blushed slightly and ran her fingers through his full beard.

"Your father has a tendency to ride with the boys most of the morning. If you're up to it, I could show you how energized I feel right now," she said playfully.

"I love you, Mrs. Phillips."

"And I you, Mr. Phillips."

Made in the USA
Lexington, KY
06 March 2012